HE NEVER CALLED AGAIN

By

Rose Quintiliano

© 2002 by Rose F. Quintiliano. All rights reserved.

No part of this book may be reproduced, stored in a retrieval system, or transmitted by any means, electronic, mechanical, photocopying, recording, or otherwise, without written permission from the author.

ISBN: 1-4033-7018-4 (e-book)
ISBN: 1-4033-7019-2 (Paperback)

This book is printed on acid free paper.

1stBooks – rev. 10/14/02

This book is dedicated with all my love to my Mom, Betty F. Quintiliano.

My Son, Brien Quintiliano Czuj and my Daughter, Kelly R.Q Olszuk.

I would also like to dedicate this book to the memory of my Dad, Jose Quintiliano.

Whose encouragement, unconditional love continues to bless me.

My grandparents, Rosa Fernandes, Jose Fernandes.

Antonio Quintiliano, Ana Quintiliano.

My Uncle, Julio Marinho.

My Aunt, Silvana Do Couto.

My Uncle, Antonio Do Couto.

My Dear Cousin, Irene Do Couto, due to unforeseen circumstances out of my control, I was unable to say "Good Night Irene" I love you, you will always be in my heart.

ACKNOWLEDGEMENTS

I thank my Mom, for helping me through this long process of writing this book and also for her patience of helping me with my children Brien and Kelly who I'm very proud of. They have showed me the meaning of really being a mother. A special thanks to the special man in my life who was my inspiration, for writing this book, without him this would never have been possible.

Above all, I thank God, for all my blessings.

I would also like to thank some of the members of my family Aunt Lucinda Marinho, Uncle Manuel Quintiliano, my cousins from Rhode Island, and Massachusetts for inspiring and believing in me. My cousins, Odette, Elaine, Anthony, Franklin, Joanne,

Rosalinda, Johnnie, Alice Fernandes, Maria Helena Fernandes, Rosa Braga, Tina Cardoso.

My Godchild, Dina.

A special thanks to Fatima Gomes, who has always been there for me.

A special thanks to Augusto Grova.

Also many thanks to Jim Mendrinos, for believing in me, and editing my first draft for pointing out what worked and what didn't. Jim you are a true inspiration for many writers.

A special thanks to my Ex-husband Janusz Czuj, who has always inspired me, and believed in me, gave me strength and courage that I will never forget.

Special thanks to one of my best friends, Donna Stiso, who has always been there for me, showing me the meaning of love, patience, and inspiration. The true meaning of success is having a friend like you. I could never thank you enough.

Special thanks also to one of my best friends, Linda Ioannides, who has also helped me in so many ways, giving me inspiration, words of wisdom, a real true friend. I could never thank you enough. I really admire you for your courage, and strong will.

Special thanks to Julio Iglesias, the pride of Spain, for making my Mom's dream a reality at the Count Basie Theatre in Red Bank, New Jersey.

Special thanks to Nikki Sorrentino, for inspiring me on the meaning of Love, you are a Shining Star.

Special thanks to Jesse Cook, whose music has brightened my soul.

I have many people in my life that have inspired me and somehow have touched my life in some special way. I would love to mention every single one of you, but it would be impossible. I think you know who you are, however I do have some special people that I would like to mention, who through some words or actions have touched my life, a sincere and heartfelt thank you.

Helen Gurley Brown, Walt Willey, Senator Torricelli, Laird Johnson, Mark Troiano, Raymond Kandola, Patricia Rodrigues, Esther Belo, Marina Campos, Luisa Fernandes, Amador Fernandes, Antonio Lopo and family, Mario Costa and family, Philipe Fernandes, Seema Fernandes, Matt Ballister, MJB Recording Studios, Jill Cagney, Maria Conchado, Narada Music, Janusz Czuj, Bartek Czuj, Jeff Toth, Irene Sanchez, Patty Iaacco, Polska Gazetta, Dean Columban, Larry Weisserman, Flo Rashbaum, Michele Rashbaum, David Brian Rashbaum, Edna Sasso, Lorraine De Benedetto, Elaine Lubas, Julia Pires,

Carlos Marques, Belinda Aquine, Mike Gonzalez, Michele Rosario, Maritza Galiano, Anabela Casimiro, Eduardo Tlatempa, Tippi Hedren, Eric Ricks, John Murray Clearwater, Pam, John, Paul Gittel, Paul Davies, D&G Limo, Dana Perone, Jeff Mayo, Yanete Barrera, Jackie Fitzpatrick, Jose Pujols, Jackie Padilla, Sovereign Bank, Starbuck's, Tony Da Silva, Edwin Rodriguez, Jim Leski, Jackie Otero and Mom, Alice Da Silva, Chris Chamberlin, Cliff Crittenten, Raul Ventura, Eli and wife, Sylvia Shellman, Delia Walling, Jessica Walling, Ginger Buiz, Carmen Sanchez, Delia Baquerizo, Pat DoSantos, Jackie Padilla, Jackie Sears, Ana Paschoal, Al Bernstein, Mickey Gilley, Johnny Lee, Kathy Laski, WKTU, 103.5 FM, Tracy Rahn, Goumba Johnny, Baltazar, and the other great DJ's on staff, Maria Fasulo, Bernie Darville, Patrick Zavist, John Deep, Russell Montecello, Manny Guillan, Nuno

Costa, Jose Leal, Samir, Mary Frey, Tony Mathias, Ela Pavlowska, RT.22 Toyota, Larry, Elizabeth Police Department, Jersey Garden's Mall, Janet Sorrentino, Basia Nej, Tammy, Barry, Liz's Hair and Nails, Gregg's Beauty Supplies, Dr. Melamedoff, Dr Jeff Glidear, Dr.Leifer, Toronto Colony Hotel, Robert Olszuk and Family, Ola Wudzinska, Mary Hagan, Friedman and Friedman Law Office, Nicky Miller, CMA, Amigos de Historia De Calahorra, Academy of Motion Pictures Arts and Science(Arlene Vidaurreta), St. Patrick's High School, Union College, Thomas M Fuller, Arshad, Kevin Mcquiness, Mike Kimm, Frank Trambino, Trax Band, (Jenkinson's Beach) Point Pleasant, Elizabeth Public Library, Union Public Library, Woodbridge Public Library, Wall Township Public Library, Flagler University, St.Augustine, Flordia, Bill Spinner, Frank Velasquez, Frank Seeley,

Lucia Costa, Leiria Bakery, Stanley, Lithuanian Bakery, Frank(Classic Coach Repair), Olga Rodrigues, Annette Burt, Denise Helfrich, Denise Daisy, Joe Orenszak, Donna and Jan, Bunny Gisondi, Andy Gisondi, Margarita Lainezsantos, Glamour Pictures, Suffern New York, Dunkin Donut's Linden, New Jersey, Jim Marketos, Bill Mckenny, Jerry Gepner, National Mobile Television, Lou Centore, Sandra Nicholas, Glenn Poll, Eugenia, Nellie Gentler, Tina Maree, Neva, Jorge Lopez, Jean Bonnet, Rafael Paredes.

A percentage of the book sales will be donated to the Leukemia Society.

AUTHOR'S NOTE

Since I always have a tendency to start something and never finish, my ultimate goal was to finish writing this book. This is my 1st book, and of course I went through all the emotions of giving birth. The emotions of self doubt, uncertainty, especially when I had to revise my first draft. I thought I was going a little crazy. I had to stop writing for a few weeks after my manuscript was revised by a friend of a friend. I had to chase the demons out of my system and then finally begin with gathering my thoughts together again. The weeding and killing off of a few characters, getting rid of the blemishes, the cut and paste of revising. I suppose the hardest part for a new writer is revising.

I began writing this about a year and a half ago, basically as just a journal, a diary of my thoughts after my trip to Spain. It started out as a history of my beginnings then somehow with a twist of events it turned into a fictional romance.

It was through my curiosity about my genealogy that led me to a small village in Northern Spain. I wanted to see for myself where a man with so much writing talent, that I admire, had been born two thousand years ago. I would like to express my appreciation, thanks and gratitude to the people of Calahorra, Spain for making my stay there so beautiful, educational and memorable, also for honoring Marco Fabio Quintiliano with such a beautiful monument, library and school. Also a special thanks to the Parador Quintiliano Hotel, for giving me the honorable key to the hotel, no words could ever express such a touching moment in my life. I will treasure it forever. Also to the fine chefs in the Hotel, that made my daughter, Kelly that special hamburger that was garnished with red peppers to create the illusion of a smiley face. She loved it.

I wanted to write something for everybody to enjoy, however it's simply impossible to captivate every person and touch every single heart. I put a lot of my heart and soul into this book, it's my first book, and at times I feel I could have done much better, but I wouldn't change a word if given the chance. I hope I entertain you, and you find it at times fun, crisp, and simply get lost in the pages.

We give to necessity the praise of virtue.

Marco Fabio Quintiliano

A liar should have a good memory.

Marco Fabio Quintiliano

Vain hopes are often like the dreams of those who wake.

Marco Fabio Quintiliano

Those who wish to appear wise among fools, among the wise are foolish.

Marco Fabio Quintiliano

We must form our minds by reading deep rather than wide.

Marco Fabio Quintiliano

One must learn to listen and listen to learn.

Rose F. Quintiliano

Only the heroes have seen the end of terror.

Rose F. Quintiliano

Dreams are beautiful and even more beautiful if they come true.

Rose F. Quintiliano

Quotations from Marco Fabio Quintiliano were researched from John Bartlett.

All characters in this book have no existence outside the imagination of the author and have no relation whatsoever to anyone bearing the same name or names. All incidents are pure invention with the exception of three places, "Help" Disco in Rio De Janeiro, and "Uncle Charlie's", and Starbuck's. These three places actually exist; therefore I am deeply indebted to the city of Rio De Janeiro, Brazil, Starbuck's and the City of Elizabeth, New Jersey.

He Never Called Again

She anxiously parked her car in Starbuck's" parking lot and waited. The bright sunlight was burning her eyes, she was feeling butterflies in her stomach. A certain queasiness was overpowering her. He was watching her from a distance in his car. She glanced at her watch; it was four in the afternoon. She patiently waited in the car for another fifteen minutes, looking around for a red sports car. Where could he be? He's late. Why am I so nervous? Where is he? Perhaps he's already inside? She came out of her car, wearing a white floral cotton dress and headed inside for the café. She was a short woman in her mid thirties, horizontally challenged. She was blonde with big innocent eyes. They were blue eyes, like the sky, clear and wide. She had to face the facts; she wasn't exactly a raving beauty. She dated on occasions; however men noticed something in her that turned them off. Was it desperation? She was thirty five, had never been married. She never had a hot, lustful affair. All she wanted out of life was to find the right guy. She wanted a husband, a child. She wanted Sex. Sweaty, hot sex. But, how do you find men, her subconscious mind whined, and wondered with the urgency of her biological clock ticking. Where can I find a man? I don't know. I've tried everything. It's the twenty first century, everyone is doing it. Why not, she thought. That's it. I'll try the internet, she thought.

Rick Jankovich sat in his car laughing and wondered why women were so vulnerable and desperate. I knew she would show up, just like a predictable woman. I can't believe how fat she is. That picture must have been taken five years ago, he thought.

He Never Called Again

It was a game to him to set meetings and never show up. He wanted to see just how far they would go. At least she didn't lie about her eyes and hair color, he thought. They had met two weeks before on the internet on a day that he was bored out of his mind. He signed in with his screen name Giant man, and entered the chatroom. His profile described him as an attractive super stud, six foot 2, and an athletic type. Who enjoyed Sunday drives to the beach, with his red corvette convertible. Romantic candlelit dinners, followed by a Broadway show, then a horse carriage ride in Central park, topped by a café latte.

Sharon Weiss was friendly and thought they interacted on the computer well, and so the emails began. Shortly after the phone numbers were exchanged he began calling her. Her voice was somewhat sexy, but that was all that was sexy about her. Rick began asking questions about her past lovers. She answered as if she was a beauty queen, full of dates and men attracted to her. Sharon was looking forward to meeting him, the night before she had laid out the outfit to wear the next day. Sharon was excited and full of anticipation.

Perhaps he was detained for some reason. What could have happened? A car accident? Little did she know that he was watching her from a distance and enjoyed seeing her desperately looking around for him.

After waiting inside for an hour she felt disappointed and hurt. I guess he's not coming, she thought. How can he do this to me? I thought he was such a nice guy. What a jerk. Sharon sipped her coffee and thought about everything that had transpired. What an asshole he is, for letting me wait here, and not even have the courtesy to call. Sharon tried calling him a few times on his cell phone, but he didn't pick up the phone the voicemail would automatically come on. She waited expectantly, but there was no sign of him. It was quite obvious that he had stood her up. With sudden decision Sharon set down her coffee cup and walked out of "Starbucks", feeling quite humiliated. What a fool I am, she thought. Perhaps he saw me and was upset that I lied about my weight.

She told herself she would handle this situation with dignity. After all it was on the computer that I met him, and she had heard so many horrific stories. It was his loss.

The door slammed shut behind her as Sharon stepped outside she noticed a man walk in that resembled his description. For a moment she hesitated. Perhaps there is a good explanation for him being late.

Oh, excuse me, Are you Rick?, she said quickly, the awkward moment creeping in. This wasn't exactly the way she had thought the initial encounter would be. She looked up at him, Sharon was a little under five foot five, and she knew that he had to be six foot two. There was a certain resemblance to the picture he had sent her through the email.

No, I'm not, he said.

I'm sorry, she finally said with her sad eyes of disappointment.

Driving home she couldn't wait to sign in on the computer and send him an email wanting some kind of explanation. She wanted to click the send button on the computer, but she felt humiliated, it was quite obvious that he had been playing with her feelings.

So much for the first encounter, she thought ruefully. A part of her wondered why anyone would be so cruel. Why did she feel so attracted to him in the first place? She wasn't quite sure. Sharon was wise enough to let it go, and decided not to bother sending him an email asking why he stood her up. She just wanted to forget about everything, the sensual emails he sent her, the feelings of lust that she felt for him. She imagined an online love affair. It was later that evening that she began to analyze the things that he said to her, the remote aloneness that she sensed in him, made her curious and lured her into the first encounter. Shaking her head over her imagination thinking that this man could have been the one, the knight and shining armor. She sank into a state of depression from what had happened in the afternoon, and hurried toward the kitchen. She headed for the refrigerator and began stuffing her face with chocolate cake. It was incredible. The taste of chocolate melting in her mouth, made her feel so much better. She turned to food for consolation. It was somewhere toward the end of the second piece of chocolate cake that Sharon realized without a doubt in her mind that Rick had no intentions of meeting her. I wonder if he had it planned all along, she thought. She took a deep breath; I need to start going places where I'm likely to meet single men, such as clubs and dances. She took another deep breath. Her brain fizzled with plans to meet men. Where are all the good men?

It was a week earlier that Rick had set up a meeting with Eva Peters at "Starbucks", she had briefly entered the chatroom and he signed on that night looking for a woman who he might seduce, someone who was easily persuaded. He began sending her instant messages and it wasn't long after that he realized that she was a frustrated housewife. Perfect, he thought. This should

He Never Called Again

be fun, watching a desperate middle-aged woman looking for romance. She will indeed meet me, for sure, he thought. Eva's private chats with him left her with much anticipated hope. So the meeting was set up and she was also disappointed and humiliated when he never showed up.

He staggers out of bed after the alarm went off at 430am. He dreaded that hour long drive to New Jersey. It had become so monotonous, fifteen years of commuting. He headed for the bathroom to release his bodily fluids. Showering the night before, it was hard for him to perk up. Gazing at the mirror, studying his handsome features with such intensity. Rick noticed that his hair was receding with each day that went by. Reaching for his pants and shirt he slowly began to dress. Grabbing his laptop he threw it in his backpack.

The drive to Jersey was sometimes met with frustrations of traffic. Arriving at the employee parking lot he was already exhausted. Rick Jankovich was indeed the classic portrait of a perfect employee. He would always arrive on time, and was very reliable. He worked as a mechanic for the corporate jets at JQ Aero Inc… He was involved in the maintainence and upkeep of the 727 aircrafts.

Rick was a tall, dark haired man in his early forties. He was a handsome, super stud with stern like features. His windows of the soul were very deep set and quite mysterious. An aura of secretive, and mystery about him. He had an inner circle of friends. Rick was the introvert personality. He began his day at work checking his personal emails and would find time to enter chat rooms. Hiding behind the computer was the only way he could express himself freely. The fear of intimacy and the lack of a social life brought him to cyber world. Entering the chat rooms with the screen name "Giant Man" made him feel like a real man. He released his anxieties by attacking women and belittling them. His observations in cyber world were that women love to be verbally abused. The lonely women in chat rooms would come back for more verbal abuse. Women are masochists, he thought. He would love to form online relationships with women using his deceiving and conning ways. Leading them on for deception. He realized that women wanted to find the so called Mr. Right. Never finding courage to actually meet them. He really didn't want to meet them. The search for excitement and thrill. Pure boredom. These women would fall for all the romantic bullshit. The callous ways he loved to control the cyber world. He knew that women grew up with the

Cinderella complex. That society instilled the fantasy in women's mind of meeting the Prince that would save them. He believed women lived in a fantasy world.

Rick was the first born to immigrant parents, who survived World War 11, and managed to settle in the Amazon jungles of Manaus. His parents were originally from Eastern Europe. His mother was the dominating controlling woman from Poland. His father was a passive man from Czech Republic. His father allowed his wife to manipulate him. It was in the early fifties that they decided to move to the land of opportunity with only three hundred dollars in their pockets. America was the hope, the dream, the salvation they thirsted for. America was a word called freedom. They were in New York. Even under the heavy clouds the city seemed to shimmer with promise. They settled in Brooklyn, living in a railroad apartment with a bathtub in the middle of the kitchen enhanced by a floral shower curtain. The two crowded rooms were filled with cots. They pressed against each other. The three year old boy's first impressions of hatred and horror were instilled in his mind. The quarrelling and vulgarity among the parents left his character morally poisoned. He remembered his mother and father, how they'd get to loving on each other sometimes in the bedroom. The sounds of his parents making love always seemed to reassure him at times. That was because the flip side of his mother's drunken rages, or the long walks his father took Rick on to escape the yelling, the fists that might come flying. He wondered if maybe all his screwing around was somehow linked to that childish idea of keeping distant. Would Rick be as messed up at fifty-six?

Would Rick believe that no woman was worth love and respect?

His parents were the inspired mobile class people striving for upper middle class. The power-monger, social strivers. At the tender age of five, they would send him to the local Mom and Pop store, Uncle Charlie's to pick up milk, and a few other things on the list.

Is anyone looking? He glanced around. He reached for the chocolate Hershey's bar and stuffed it in his right pocket. Walking back home, he began devouring the tasty chocolate bar, that melted in his mouth. That was easy, he thought.

Growing up, he began forming a pit bull personality. His sadistic hatred for animals was seen at the age of twelve when he threw his neighbor's cat out the window. The resentment stages were beginning to build up. He felt deprived of his childhood years. He despised his siblings, Martina, Isabella, and Natalie. He was quite content being the only child. He was later forced to share the attention and the little love that was given to him. Growing up his hatred for his sisters grew intensely throughout the years. He found himself surrounded by women and shoes. He had lost all respect for his father since he would never stand up to his mother. He didn't look up to his father as many young boys do, since his Mother was the dictator. He looked at him as weak and pathetic. At times he would silently think, if only she was my wife. I would smack her across the face. He felt the anguish of being in a dysfunctional family. He felt he was different from his sisters. He was blamed for everything, since he was the oldest sibling.

Rick's upbringing made him parsimonious, cold and calculating. He grew up as many boys do with an identity crisis, unable to separate the discovery of his own temperament. His mother would leave him alone at night with his father so she could go out drinking with her friends. She loved the night life. Many times he would be awoken in the darkness of the night, catching a glimpse of his Mother inebriated and stumbling to her room. Minutes later the shouting began. You are useless, she would scream. I never should have married you, she yelled. He would overhear her boisterous mouth. He began to see her as an overbearing, drunken witch. The troubled relationship between his parents was unbearable to him. Rick's mother had such smothering control. Rick vowed he would never let a woman control him. She had such overwhelming demands on the children. He missed his mother's nature to protect and nurture. He began to see his mother in a different light. She was a ruthless woman.

Rick would go after school hanging out on the street corners with the other delinquents. He began to learn how to con people. Learning manipulation, and becoming a pathological liar. Through his teenage years he became a dark, pessimistic shroud, even though he was showered with common sense and experience. He was lacking substance and character. He became a rebel, a unique mind searching for the truth. A loner with a raging anger boiling inside him ready to explode. In his school years he began pushing and fighting with the other boys. Rick was a bully in high school. Stealing things from the other students and lying about it, below average grades, picking fights. He just didn't care. Overindulging in pleasure seeking behavior. What evil lurked inside of him? His parents had one last attempt that was to enroll him in a private school. The school was costly, but not a heavy price to pay for a child's education. They didn't want to see him wasting his life away. The rigid rules and regulations perhaps would either break him or make him. Rick had to maintain certain above average grade. So he used his bully ways to get the students to help him with the homework. It was in his junior year in High school that he would feel the pain. The real pain of helplessness. Two days before Christmas vacation. Rick and his other delinquent friends decided to ice skate in the local park. Ignoring the signs, do not skate. He felt he was a daredevil. Invincisible. He began to perform. He fell into a crack. It was minutes later the call was placed to his mother from the police car. She was required to give her permission to take him to the hospital. The emergency room was filled with so many people. He was in so much pain. The minutes turned into hours. The Doctor was very busy since it was the holiday season and they were understaffed. Rick waited patiently. Suddenly the white curtain was abruptly pushed back and finally the Doctor began to speak to him. The Doctor began examining him. Rick knew it was quite serious. He couldn't move his leg. The fall on the ice, sounded like a tree branch cracking in half. He knew it was fractured. I'm so unlucky, he silently thought. The force of destiny. Why? he thought. He was out of commission for the next eight long weeks. He was faced with the possibility of surgery on his leg. He began to panic. The pain was excruciating. Rick was strong. No pain, he thought. No tears. I am a man, and real men don't cry. With his leg in a cast he walked out of the hospital hours later in crunches. He slowly began going into a state of depression. He was full of hostility. Rick began to withdraw further into his own empty shelled world. Rick just didn't care. He didn't care about his life, homework or school. He was raged with anger. He began to search deep into his empty soul. He felt the world should pity him. Returning to school he felt the teachers would be lenient and give him a break. The real world was beginning to teach him a valuable lesson. He failed three subjects and he was dismissed. Rick struggled with hot, muggy days walking to summer school. The challenges he faced to pass the three subjects. The days of hanging out with the hoodlums and misfits had suddenly awakened him. Suddenly he came to realize he was backed into a corner. Unable to gain special pleasure in plagiarizing, swindling or extorting homework form his fellow students. This time he was on his own, he had no choice. He had to survive the summer school program and pass. It was after he passed his summer school program that he decided to retaliate. It was after school, no one was in the classroom. Perfect, he thought. He took a few pages from his English book, starting ripping them up in throwing them in the wastepaper basket. He strikes a match, and slipped it in the basket. The glow of the fire begins to bounce off his face. Rick begins to walk briskly.

I did it.

That's for all the days that I had to sweat it out, he thought.

I hope the school burns down.

They deserve it. My summer vacation is ruined.

Walking home, laughing, he began to hear sirens getting closer, heading for the school.

Rose F. Quintiliano

He wanted to go back in September, to St. Vincent's private school. The rules were meant to be broken, and perhaps they can be persuaded to accept me back in school, he thought. He turned to his Mother. He knew she was a very determined and persistent woman. Mrs. Jankovich finally met with the principal of the school. She cried and pleaded for her son. She knew that if he wasn't accepted back in school. All hope was gone. He would become a lost empty soul. He managed to finish high school with his manipulative ways.

He had to prove his manhood, since he didn't have a strong father figure. The stages of long hair to his waist, then the shorter pony tail look. Proving his manhood with Harley bikes and penis extension cars. To strengthen his warped, racist mind he read books on World history, military tactics with extreme strategic measures. The in-depth knowledge he had of the World War 2 bombers. He was able to debate in conversations the Avro 683 Lancaster. His fascination with the four 1223-kw Rolls Royce Merlin. He knew about its maximum speed of 287 mph. The power it had to target and back even with two engines down. He viewed the world in black and white. The world to him was in concrete. Rick mastered the Hitler's regime with many hours spent reading his favorite book Mein Kampf.

His idea of a perfect world would be the Taliban regime. He always resented his parents for lacking the financial funds to enroll him in College. His only choice would be to enroll in the military. It was there that he mastered neutrality. They would find his weaknesses and break him down. Then slowly they began to build up his confidence to his potential.

It was very easy for him to maintain several sexual relationships even in the Air Force. He derived great pleasure in discussing his sexual exploits and conquests with his buddies. His inner circle. His arrogant tone of voice boasting about his latest conquest was overheard by his base commander. Rick was telling his buddy Steve how this woman was all over him. She just couldn't get enough of him. He was describing her in detail. Mona was a woman in her late thirties, she was slender, with hazel eyes, but had a sad haunted look in her eyes. She confided in Rick that her husband was impotent. She longed to have a real man unlock the passions in her. Rick described the butterfly tattoo she had on her inner thigh. The base commander's face suddenly turned red, and with a lions roar screamed out Rick Jankovich follow me. He suddenly looked back and remembered that night when

He Never Called Again

he was on night duty with Air defense alert aircraft. Rick was the crew chief in a fighter squadron. The officer commanding and squadron commander had come earlier just after sunset for the acceptance of the aircraft and later the OC directed the crew chief on duty to Top Up the aircraft with fuel. That specific night at about 11, Rick and another crew chief were all on alert with their duties when the ADA siren started blowing to announce the scramble. The pilots ran towards their aircraft but the two crew chiefs reached the aircraft before them. They quietly went through the star up drill and within moments saw the aircraft off. When the aircraft passed close to him, Rick noticed that fuel was flowing freely from it's overboard drain. Rick tried to quickly run after the aircraft but to no avail. Luckily the squadron engineering officer saw his terrified plight and rushed to his assistance in his jeep.

Rose F. Quintiliano

He asked what is the problem. With the roaring sounds of the aircraft engines, Rick tried to hand signal it to be stopped. The squad engineer officer picked the crew chief up in his vehicle and drove alongside the aircraft. They finally managed to reach the aircraft just prior to brake release and motioned the pilot to hold the take off. Rick managed to crawl under the aircraft and to his terrifying horror discovered that the refueling handle was down. Apparently the afternoon crew chief had forgotten to raise the handle after refueling the aircraft. Rick signaled the pilot to return to the Pen. The pilot complied and took the standby aircraft after patting the crew chief on the back. If that aircraft had taken off, the fuel flowing from it's overboard drain would have reached the after burner flame and a huge fire would have resulted. The pilot would have to eject and the USF would have suffered a loss of a precious aircraft.

It was the very next evening that the Commander was dining out with his wife and he noticed Rick. He congratulated him and introduced him to his wife Mona. Gazing into his eyes, she secretly desired him. It was shortly after that introduction, she began plotting ways to meet him accidentally. The next day she nonchalantly walked by him and began a conversation. He knew by looking in her eyes that she was a desperate, lonely woman, craving love and attention.

His future career as a pilot in the Air force was short lived. Rick's promiscuous sexual behavior led him to be dishonorably discharged. Rick continued his education at night in hopes of someday becoming a pilot; he had his AP license as an aircraft technician. He was content being a mechanic. He blamed his loss of ambition on this evil woman that destroyed his career. He felt life wasn't fair.

It was during one of his traffic bound commutes to work that he began thinking of his ex-wife and flashbacks of his life. The commute was mechanical, but the salary was substantial.

He was approaching his 28th birthday, with social and family pressures he decided to marry Donna. He knew that she had been acting aloof lately. In every relationship there would reach a point of decision making. He seemed infatuated with her. Rick wanted to settle down and perhaps start a family. He was tired of the one niters. His Don Juan lifestyle. Perhaps it was peer pressure. He expected Donna to fit the mold, of an ideal wife. He was given an ultimatum by her. She wanted like every woman to be married and have a child. The fairytale love. The prince to save her. The dreams of wearing a white, wedding dress. The thrill of being the center of attention, a special day. The anticipation of marriage, love that will last forever. They were both in their twenties and the illusion of marriage made sense. The innocence of entering an institution blindfolded. Rude awakening for the believers. Everything was bliss in the beginning, just like a new euphoric romance. The honeymoon stages. The dancing on clouds.

Donna Sims, was a petite woman, with long blonde hair. Her eyes were sky blue. She was in her early twenties when she first met Rick. It was on a hot, sunny muggy day, when he walked in to pay his water bill. Donna was working at the water company. She captured his attention with the short black skirt with a slit on the left side and low cut blouse, showing her cleavage. It was his main attraction. Fearing rejection he moved in on her very slowly. He began to plot. Watching her from afar. He knew that she took her lunch breaks at noon. Casually meeting her outside on her lunch break. Even though he was a bit timid, fearing rejection. He finally made his calculated move. After a brief fifteen minutes of idle conversation, he realized she was weak and could easily be persuaded to go out with him. After weeks of stalking her, he finally had the courage to ask her for a date. Donna was the giving, nurturer type. It didn't take long for Rick to realize that she was insecure and showed signs of low self esteem. He was brilliant in his master plan. After a year of dating he decided to tie the knot. Rick and Donna were married at two in the afternoon on the third of March. It was a big, beautiful ceremony celebrated in St. Luke's Church. Donna wore a white gown with a massive train and thousands of tiny seed pearls. It was beautiful; it was more than she ever dreamed of.

Rick hadn't cared about the ceremony; a simple wedding in City Hall would have served him fine. This was all for her. It was her fairy tale. Donna was living every woman's fairy tale. Rick was her prince who had swept her away into the land of happily ever after. Honeymoons could not last forever, but she believed in her heart that they would never fall out of love.

The service was quite beautiful. She heard every single word. Promising to love and to cherish until death do them part. Donna's hand trembled when he slipped the wedding band on her finger; she noticed his hand was steady and firm. The priest finally proclaimed them husband and wife, and the happiness that she felt was almost elevating.

Rick lifted her veil and took her in his arms and kissed her. Everyone began to applaud. Gazing into each others eyes they turned to travel back up the aisle. He swept her in his arms and pulled her tight against him, his dark mysterious eyes were full of love and amusement.

Oh Rick, I love you so much,

I really do.

He bent and kissed her passionately, as they stepped into the limousine. The guests were in the lavish hotel ballroom as they pulled up in the limousine. Handshaking and kissing, welcoming friends and guests lasted about thirty minutes. The bride, groom and members of their immediate families were seated at a long table in the front while their other guests were placed at round tables for ten. The white and pink damask cloths gleamed with silver and crystal. The room was filled with roses that filled the air with a delicious scent. Just before the wedding cake was served, the waiters came out with a parade of ice sculptures in the forms of hearts. Then the six- layer cake was wheeled out and Donna and Rick cut the first slice. After several more toasts the band struck up for the dancing. When Donna and Rick walked onto the dance floor the guests began to clap. They made such a gorgeous couple.

Suddenly it was midnight. Donna and Rick were spending their wedding night in the hotel suite. Instead, after leaving under a shower of rice, they carefully circled the hotel and then turned off the car's lights, came down the hotel's driveway leading to the garages. Giggling and laughing like mischievous conspirators, they tiptoed through the hotel's hall and up the elevator to the tenth floor.

Rose F. Quintiliano

Rick opened the Hotel's door and carried Donna over the threshold. When he put her down, she looked at the honeymoon suite. A small fire glowed, warming the cool March night. The maids left a bucket of champagne by the bed and turned down the spread, revealing the white satin comforter.

Rick popped the cork on the bottle of champagne and poured Donna a glass.

To you, Baby. I hope our life together will always be as happy as tonight. As he spoke Rick honestly believed his words were the truth.

I hope so Rick, she said, toasting his glass with hers.

They sipped the champagne in front of the fire in silence. When they finished the glass, Rick went into the bathroom. Donna was twisting and turning, trying to get at the buttons at the back of her gown. There was only one thing on her mind. She managed to free one shoulder and then the other. Finally she had slipped out of her white beaded gown and into her white lace teddy.

She was nervous as she laid in the huge king size bed waiting for Rick. The fire illuminated his face as he bent over her and kissed her lips. She began embracing him, and they made passionate love. Rick awoke early the next morning and just watched Donna sleep. I can't believe I actually married her, he thought. Donna began to stretch and slowly began to open her eyes.

Did you sleep well? he asked.

Yes, like a newborn baby.

Marriage is such an institution, Rick thought. Knowing he had to be committed, gave him an eerie feeling. I'll have to sleep with her, every night, he thought.

You've made me so happy Rick, she said. It was almost ten o'clock in the morning. They decided to take a shower together. Donna wanted to believe that Rick had fallen in love with her, but insecurities began to creep in. I hope in time you will really love me, she said.

You're beautiful, he said and I do love you.

A couple of hours later the limousine came to pick them up to take them to the airport. After checking in at the ticket counter, they turned to head for the gate, where they sat and waited for their plane to board.

Rick and Donna were to catch a plane for the Grand Cayman, forty five minutes later they were sitting comfortably in their seats, when a voice came on the intercom.

He Never Called Again

Good Afternoon, Ladies and Gentlemen.

This is Captain Johnson. The weather in Grand Cayman is 87 degrees. The flight will take an estimated three hours and fifty minutes. It looks like we'll have clear skies. We'll talk to you again once we have reached our cruising altitude. We hope you will enjoy your flight and if there is anything we can do to make your flight more pleasant, let us know. Welcome Aboard.

It was later that afternoon that they arrived in Grand Cayman, it lived up to their dreams; it was a place for lovers. The first night she stood out on the balcony of the hotel watching the moonlight.

Donna?

Rick's voice called out.

Enjoying the view?

Yes, baby, this is so beautiful and romantic. The weather is so warm, I love this place. She walked over and found him in bed. Another night of passion reached new heights. Early the next morning, Donna slipped out of bed and dressed, and went downstairs to the lobby. She wanted a cup of coffee, so she walked into the dining room. Then she took her coffee upstairs back to the hotel room. As she entered their room, she found Rick had just finished dressing.

Where the hell where you?

From now on Donna, if you're going to leave the room, let me know.

Were you worried Rick?

I was a bit concerned.

Where were you anyway?

Downstairs, I went to get coffee.

Don't you ever leave the room without telling me.

He Never Called Again

Alright, she said.

Did you have to call your lover?

What lover? She said

I have no lover; you are the one I love.

She began to notice a change in him, but she didn't want anything to spoil the honeymoon. Rick had called for room service. There was a knock on the door, it was the bellboy. It wasn't long after he lifted the silver dome that covered their bacon and eggs, and he began serving himself. Rick began observing her pushing her eggs around the plate rather than eating them.

Why don't you eat?

You better hurry up.

We are going scuba diving remember.

Yes, I know.

I didn't forget.

The silence that followed her last words went on so long that Donna was certain he was angry at her.

Rick began laughing.

It was after one o'clock they had plans to scuba dive. They were looking forward to it; they both enjoyed the adventures of scuba diving. The sensation excited her. A few hours later they went for a swim; there was something deliciously sensuous about the flow of the water, the movement of the ripples through her legs. Her fingers and the movement of the water were almost unendurable. Rick moved his body away and kissed her. Their heads went under water, and they separated, each struggling to gain balance. Laughing and coughing and choking, they headed for the beach. Rick suddenly grabbed her and kissed her. I can't stop touching you.

They had no towels. They didn't want to sit wet in the sand. They looked at each other. Let's go back to the Hotel, said Rick. They slogged back through the sand, arms wrapped up around each other. They were in a hurry. The teasing and caresses and sensations were building up.

When they reached the hotel room, Rick slid open the drapes so that the room was filled with glorious sunlight. Donna was in the bathroom with the door closed. Rick heard the shower running and opened the door.

Rick moved to the shower stall and joined her. She was glistening with soap. He held her to him, running his hands up and down over the slippery surface of her suntanned skin.

She looked at him and smiled. He crushed her to him; he was hard as a rock. His hands cupped her bottom and pressed it harder to him. Rick held her for a moment, and then he took the soap and moved his hands between her legs. I've done that already. So what, I'll do it again. He continued with the soap up her legs.

The sensation was building up faster. Donna took the soap from his hand and began doing the same. That's enough, and he suddenly moved away from her.

What's wrong?

He turned on the cold water, and they began to gasp. He turned it off, and opened the glass door and they stepped out.

Donna reached for the white towel and started drying herself. She tried to dry him off at the same time, but they got tangled up in arms and legs and towels. Perhaps we should do it ourselves. She stood there looking at him for a moment, when suddenly she dropped to her knees and began kissing every inch of his body. They moved out of the steamy bathroom to the sunlit bedroom.

Rick pulled the curtains closed so that the sun would not be in their eyes. When he turned back around, she was lying in bed. He joined her in bed. She raised herself on her hands and slid over so that her breasts were above his face. After a minute she swung her leg over and straddled him and guided him to her. Rick began to experience a strange sense of control and power. It was exciting to him, the way he had such control over her. Rick felt that it could go on forever. The extreme control he felt added pleasure in performance to pleasure in the act. Why was this happening to me, he thought. Was it hostility, resentment, a desire to frustrate and disappoint? For a moment there was a desire to exploit this control, to revel in it. Rick looked at her face, in total concentration, with eyes tightly closed. Imagining what?

Rick laid there conscious of the power to give her pleasure. He almost smiled at her determination to press on to her completion, aware all over again that sex is selfish, impulsive, calculated, colored by all the hues of each personality. There was something demanding in Donna. He wondered how she can say, I love having you inside of me.

Donna was intense when it came to sex, she would become frustrated if she didn't achieve climax. She came in a series of short brief climaxes. Rick knew that she was through, and even though he controlled himself, he pretended. He was laughing inside, pretending! In a few moments Rick began to withdraw. He looked over Donna's shoulder, and he suddenly wanted to be alone. A few more days of this honeymoon, he thought.

The trip home was exhausting; they felt drained, tired and listless. The first month was spent exploring under the hood. He was getting restless in the iron four poster bed in the gothic bedroom. Rick was becoming bored, he needed stimulation. Donna realized after the third month she had made a huge mistake. The reality had sunk in, she was destined to be a maid and cook. Donna knew that Rick had changed. It didn't matter how much attention and love he received from her. He became secretive and full of suspicion. He imagined deceptive conditions were working against him. Pure imagination. The depths of deception were not genuine; he couldn't learn to be more pliable. Selfish love. He knew deep down inside of him, he loved no one. He loved only himself. The romance was dying.

Her short lived days of dining out were gone. He became a dominating tyrant, a typical old fashioned lord of the manor. He was very difficult to live with, so irritable. His violent tempers and mood swings were driving her crazy. Donna couldn't take it any more living in the basement apartment with her crazy in laws. His mother was always there meddling. The lunatic sisters were always instigating problems.

Donna began to resent that she would walk in the apartment after work and Mrs. Yankovich would be inspecting the house for dust. Hello, Mrs. Yankovich, smiled Donna. Good Afternoon, replied Mrs. Yankovich. Donna, I changed the curtains for you, said Mrs. Yankovich. I just put them up last week, replied Donna. They didn't look clean, angrily Mrs. Yankovich responded. Donna couldn't believe the nerve of that arrogant woman. She was fighting a losing battle. She simply couldn't win. It had to be her way, or no way, Donna thought. Between his mother and his meddling sisters she had to find away to move out. Rick knew that the house across the street was up for sale. He decided to buy it. Perhaps that bitch will stop bothering me, complaining about my mother and sisters everyday, Rick thought. Finally, Donna thought she would have privacy. Donna didn't realize that Rick gave the spare key to the house to his mother, so she could stop by anytime. Mrs. Yankovich knew that Donna was weak. She knew that she could control her too. The house was a modern contemporary, well decorated house out in the suburbs of Long Island. It was shortly after moving in, that Donna wanted to have the family room painted in a classic off white color. She had to wait for the weekend so Rick could ask his parents to come over and help since he was physically exhausted from the commute.

Donna continued working at the water company after she was married. She thought that she was going to quit her job after her marriage to Rick. She thought wrong. There was no way in hell he would allow her to stay home and watch soap operas.

Donna continued to work full time, cook and clean for him, and be a slut in bed. She wanted quality time with him. Rick just wanted to work and come and go as he pleased. She would start to prepare dinner as she arrived home. She would have the table set, the hours would go by, and sometimes he just wouldn't show up at all. She began to actually see how selfish he really was. The seldom rare days that he was tired and came home directly from work, she began realizing how selfish he really was.

He Never Called Again

Rick are you hungry? asked Donna.

No, I already ate at work, replied Rick.

How inconsiderate of you, Donna shouted.

The fighting would begin and he would remember the times his parents were always fighting, the quarrels that would never end. Donna began plotting ways for him to stay home. She loved to keep Rick busy with the household chores. Rick the living room has to be painted, she would say. It was after that painting weekend that he began to slowly withdraw from her. Exhausted from his 14 hour shift and Friday commute, he asked his parents to come over the weekend to help. His parents were exhausted from helping them paint. It was on Monday night, after his parents left that she wanted to get kinky and paint each other. Donna wanted to dip her hands in the paint and leave handprints on his body. She wanted to explore his body. Rick wasn't in the mood. Gasping heavily with anger, he zeroed in on Donna as if she was a target and shouted with a cry of the dammed,

What?!

His scream rattled the ceiling fan. In the silence that followed a lone paint chip drifted, lazily down from one of the cracked hinges shaken down by his invocation. It was that isolated incident that would trigger the cruel mental mind games.

What a bitch, he thought.

You women just don't understand, said Rick. He just wasn't in the mood, he just wanted to finish the job and call it quits for the night.

I just want some fun, said Donna.

Fun, he said. Rick raised his hand and smacked her across the face. With tears falling down her face, she felt so humiliated. That was his purpose. The tactics. The strategy of control. He first began accusing her of cheating on him, at that moment he remembers the day he went to the Titi bar, he was sitting there on the bar stool with his friend. He ordered a beer, looking up at the dancer he began thinking and plotting of ways to get her. Rick began to wonder.

Oh my God, she is so hot.

She is beautiful.

God, how I want her.

How can I get her?

What can I possibly do?

Perhaps it will take a few hundred dollars?

Money that's what she probably wants, he thought.

No, I'll try to charm her.

I'll tell her how beautiful she is.

I'll tell her she's the most beautiful woman that I've seen in my life.

Fantasizing, plotting. He began going there everyday after work. He became a regular. He knew all the dancers by name. A few weeks later, dressed in his Armani suit, with his Italian silk tie, the look of stepping out of a magazine layout for "Gentlemen's Quarterly" he charmed his way to be introduced to the dancer after slipping the bartender a twenty dollar bill. That same evening, with a couple of hundred dollars, he found himself at the local motel, with the dancer.

Debbie was drop dead gorgeous, with a statuesque, muscular body and flawless perfect face. He wrapped Debbie in a crushing embrace and covered her mouth with his hungry, insistent kisses. A low moan escaped him and his hands began to move over her body. The feel of his length of his hard, lean body against her flesh caused her passion to flame like wild fire. A raging fire swept through her body, spreading from every point where he touched her. Every men's fantasy to sleep with a dancer, he thought. As Rick eased himself into her, a spiral of fiery pleasure radiated through her body.

"This might hurt a little", he whispered in her ear, but she was too deep in the toils of her need to heed any kind of warning. She clung to him, pressing his firm buttocks to her, trying to draw him within her to reach her rampaging need and desire. A sharp pain momentarily penetrated the blanket of sensual delight that enveloped her, but then she experienced the wonder of his bigness deep within her, filling her with his heat and desire, and all memory of pain was wiped from her mind. Rick and his friend Tony had become regulars at the bar.

Tony Torres was his unhappily married friend. He was Rick's accomplice. Tony was also in his forties, good looking with almost perfect features. His hair was black and wavy, long enough to curl at the base of his neck. A certain debonair, movie star quality in him.

Tony was miserable, but he stayed in his loveless marriage for the kid's sake. He knew that if he ever left his wife she would use the children as pawns. He would be taken to the cleaners. Sleeping in the backseat of his burgundy van. Even though Rick hated the lowlife Spanish minorities. Rick considered Tony his friend. He needed Tony. Rick enjoyed listening to his womanizing ways. The only difference between them was that Tony loved women with huge derrieres and Rick loved the bosom types. At times they would takes bets to see if the dancer would fall for Rick. It was a game between them. A week later he wanted Debbie again, but she was busy with another client from the bar, so he found himself going home and fantasizing about her in the shower, where he began to slowly stroke and imagine she was there with him.

Through the bitter years Rick began to wear Donna down; he would walk into the kitchen and see her wearing sweat pants and be turned off. Where was the 125 pound woman that I married, he thought. He systematically humiliated her. Preying on her weaknesses. So many weeks and months went by that he would walk in from work and would just ignore her. He ignored her existence of a human being; the flicking of the remote channel was his idea of annoying her, irritating her. Rick would deprive her of sex. He would punish her. His first tactics were the verbal abuse. Then he began smacking her around. They had one thing in common that kept the marriage alive. That was the mutual love for scuba diving. She desperately tried to salvage the marriage. Perhaps a change of scenery will enhance the romance, she thought. She began planning a trip to Grand Cayman, perhaps a second honeymoon. The hotel was quite luxurious and they found themselves wrapped up in each others arms every night that weekend, it was the last attempt on her part. She secretly planned to trap him. A month after the trip she was quite excited. She went to the bathroom and reached for the final test. It had two horizontal pink lines in the window. Donna was scared and confused. They were somewhat bohemians, but it was that fateful night that she finally came to the realization that the marriage wasn't what she anticipated. That same evening she was waiting for him to come home. The candlelit dinner was set. The sexy outfit from Frederick's of Hollywood was quite alluring. She wanted to capture the moment. The right moment to tell him. The key slowly turns and he walks

He Never Called Again

in exhausted from a long day at work. Rick, can I get you a drink, she said. Alright I'll have a vodka and tonic, he responded. She slowly walks over to the bar and began pouring the absoult vodka. Handing him the glass. Rick I have something to tell you. She sat next to him and began to hug him. I'm pregnant, smiling she said.   What, he shouted. I thought you were on protection, angrily he said. I was but remember our trip to the Grand Cayman last month. I simply forgot to take it that night, she said. We just bought this house; we can't afford a baby now. It's not the right time, he said. He knew that if she had the baby, that he would be trapped forever. He slowly began persuading her to get an abortion.

An Abortion, shouting she said.

No Way, Donna exploded. Rick pleaded with her to be reasonable.

I don't think you love me.

How in the world do you expect me to believe you love me, if you don't want me to have your baby? Rick went into a rage. He finally said either you have this baby without me, or get an abortion and we will stay together. The discussion went on for days. He was determined to win. She finally became exhausted from listening to his tyrant voice. Things would never be the same between them, she thought. I really hate him, she silently thought. Donna had to wait a few weeks more to schedule the abortion. Things would never be the same between them. I hate him, I despise him, she silently thought. Weeks went by, her morning sickness was increasing. She would reach for the saltine crackers by her bed. She had to hold on to her sanity. Rick had little empathy for her. Holding her hand to her mouth she would run to the bathroom to throw up.

Slut, Slut, silently he thought. Does she really expect me to feel sorry for her? He was like an East German guard, without feelings, or remorse. Donna began looking through the yellow pages for abortion clinics. She finally found one and began dialing the number. She scheduled an appointment; it was only at nine weeks that they could perform the abortion. The days and weeks seemed forever. The crackers diminished the nausea, but they really didn't help. The day finally arrived, she asked her Mother to go with her to the clinic. Rick was so unmoved by the whole ordeal that he wanted nothing to do with the procedure. Donna was frightened, ashamed. What if someone sees me in here, she silently thought. The guilt feelings of terminating a child were driving her crazy. She didn't want to lose Rick. She wanted the baby. She didn't have a choice; he had made that quite clear. Donna knew that if she went full term, he would have left her. In the waiting room of the clinic, she turned to her Mother. Mommy, I'm so scared, sighed Donna. Don't worry sweetie, everything will be alright, replied her Mother. Reality had finally set in. A husky voice called out. Mrs.Yankovich, shouted the nurse. Come with me, said the nurse. Donna hesitantly stood up and followed her into the dressing room. Now take off your clothes and put on this gown, said the nurse. Alright, replied Donna. Tears falling down her eyes, she knew the moment had finally arrived. She didn't even pay attention to the introduction of the Doctor. Silently she thought, this is who will kill my child. It will be over in five minutes, said the doctor. Lying down, the sounds of a vacuum suction, was what she remembered. It felt like someone was tearing my insides out, Donna thought. She stood the pain without general anesthesia. It was finally over it seemed like forever. She finally managed to get up, and walk out of the room as quickly as she could. A room full of sad memories. She walks very slowly to the dressing room where she left her jeans and black tank top. She takes her hand and touches her stomach. Gone! Gone! The baby is gone, she thought. She would never be the same. A depressed state of mind. On minute I'm pregnant, and then I'm not. The feelings of guilt would haunt her forever. Mom, she cries out. It's alright baby, said her Mother. You will be alright, responded her Mother. Let's go for lunch, said her Mom. I'm not hungry, said Donna. A little soup will make you feel better, said her Mom. Alright! Sighed Donna.

That evening was spent with feelings of guilt and remorse. The feelings that would last for months. A memory that would never be forgotten. The resentment that she felt for Rick would never go away. She tried to forgive him, but she would never forget how inhumane he was. It was about six months later that she found herself pregnant again. It was on one of his weekend drinking binges. She wanted her marriage to work. She didn't want to be consider a failure in marriage also. Donna purposely forgot to use protection again. She was determined to keep the baby this time. She wanted to trap Rick. Reliving the same nightmare once before. She had to confront him. The scenario she planned was to catch him by surprise. Hoping this time he would have a change of heart. He finally came home that evening from work and walked to the bathroom. She knew in her heart that whenever he walked through the door and went straight to the bathroom. She knew he had been with another woman. Her woman's intuition

He Never Called Again

sensed something wrong. She continued setting the table. He finally walked out of the bathroom and noticed she was smiling. I am pregnant again, said Donna. His face dropped and said, No, No. Not again, shouted Rick. What is the problem now? Money is still tight, yelled Rick. Donna walked to the kitchen and at that precise moment she knew, he was destroying her physically and mentally. She finally had given up all hope. A year later she had to relive the nightmare over again, she silently thought. No, not this time, she was determined to have the child. She wanted this baby. Her biological clock was ticking away. She was approaching her 32nd birthday. She wanted to feel like a woman experiencing childbirth. She didn't feel complete. She wanted to feel the movements. The kicking! She wanted a new life growing inside of her.

Donna was in her seventh week, when he began to argue with her that Fourth of July weekend. The voices began to rise, the temperaments were flying. She was upstairs outside the bedroom when he suddenly pushed her down the stairs. She lands on her stomach. She begins to feel the cramps, they were heavy. She felt excruciating pain. The crampy feelings of a heavy period. Blood kept on gushing. She felt like she was hemorrhaging. The pain was severe. She walks slowly to the bathroom by the foyer and the blood continued gushing, the cramps were intensifying. Rick had no other choice but to rush her to the hospital.

Donna, I'm so sorry, it was an accident, said Rick. I didn't mean to hurt you, please forgive me, said Rick. He continued with his false promises. Rick promised Donna it would never happen again. Donna spent the whole night crying in the hospital bed. The nurses were consoling her. She began to think he would never change. She was fighting a losing battle. Donna was released the very next day. The depression was setting in again. The feelings of emptiness, had overpowered her. She began to withdraw. The feelings for him were diminishing. He had chipped away little by little any feelings of love. Donna felt the loneliness, the lack of attention from Rick.

She decided to go back to work. She was very depressed for the first few weeks. My life is wasting away, she thought. She kept to herself. Towards the end she started looking at children in the playground. A disturbing mixture of hate with a feeling of love and sweetness.

It was a few weeks later, that she forced herself to go back to work, and she began to notice Matthew. He would ask if she wanted to go out for lunch. At first, she just wanted to be left alone, but then she finally said yes. The sun was shining; it was a perfect summer day. She was very quiet at first. She slowly began to open up to Matthew. She found a friend in her co-worker. Matthew Dyers was a very empathic, supportive man. He was in his mid thirties. He was tall, blond with that California, laid back look. He was the athletic type. He was single. Matthew was quite the charmer with his hazel, hypnotic eyes. He began encouraging and charming Donna in so many ways.

Donna, you look so beautiful today.

Oh, thanks Matt.

You have the most beautiful eyes, I've ever seen.

Your hair looks great.

Thanks.

Donna, accepted the compliments graciously, and glanced away. She had washed her hair earlier that morning and it gleamed like gold in the hot afternoon sun. He really tried to force his mind off sex, but it was hard. He was falling for her.

After seven tortuous years with Rick, finally she had found salvation. A real man. Donna began having a special friendship with Matthew, the secret meetings, the lunches; it was quite innocent at first. He encouraged her to further her education, to study computer programming. She found in Matthew everything that Rick was lacking. She found compassion, encouragement, attention.

Rick continued with his womanizing ways. He would stop at the titi bar with Tony almost every night. He felt comfortable there. He was reliving his perverted fantasies. He would fantasize about going up there on stage and cupping the dancer's breasts, and taking off his pants and doing her right there on stage. He wanted to conquer everything that walked. The thrill of the chase. The conquest/ trophy attitude. He loved watching and being watched. Then his mind would turn to the other fantasies of having a few other guys join in. He loved to watch the dancers flash at him. It turned him on. Rick thought he would continue his routine forever. Even though he was married he was still uncommitted, he felt as though he had walked into a small dark room, a black box he didn't like, half of him felt trapped and boxed. He was married less than six months when he began his cheating ways. Rick began to sleep around with other women on a regular basis. He believed he would continue his womanizing ways forever.

He Never Called Again

Over the years Donna had tried to muster enough self-respect to divorce him, but it was always easier to dull things with a glass of wine. She hated him with a fierceness that ate at her like acid. Donna kept trying to adjust and accommodate. She resented him for always looking at other woman the rare seldom times they went out. Her jealousy was well-founded because he literally slept with dozens of them. Rick despised her dependency. For the most part, she wanted the marriage to continue and he wanted it to end. He was with women all the time. She would ask him to be home before dawn, and he would go out with other women and be home after dawn. They would fight, and he would apologize. He would say he would change, but he didn't. He didn't know what that meant. He didn't know how to change. He figured it would somehow prevent himself from doing what he wanted to do. He always had a need to wander, not just sexually, but in every way. He didn't like the sense of being pinned down in one spot.

Donna didn't neglect Rick, for no matter what she did during the day, she was always home by six to shower and dress provocatively for him. Their friends considered them the ideal couple. When Rick became bored he showed his feelings with prolonged silence. He would watch Donna's routine with envy.

Rick was jealous of Donna's tranquility at times. He began reading the paper one Sunday afternoon in September, while Donna began preparing dinner. It was fall, the trees were changing, and life was racing by. Stepping outside, he felt his feelings of frustration growing, he needed some fresh air.

He felt trapped, and to complicate matters, he wasn't sure he really wanted to leave. Rick needed at times the security of a woman's love, his conflict was deepening. He felt like the claustrophobic stuck in the elevator. Why did he let Donna control his life? He had to answer to her, he hated that. After staring at the trees for a few minutes, he walked back inside the house, tossing down the paper, he walked upstairs. He stood observing the room. Maybe a change of routine would put him in a better mood, he thought. He hated being married, the idea of always telling her where he was going. When are you coming back home, drove him crazy. He wanted out, but how? Clenching his fists, he tried to control his temper. Donna did her best to try to make him happy, including waiting on him hand and foot. Donna was quick to note that he just wanted to be left alone. Still she heard herself asking, "Rick are you going to have dinner?"

I'll be down in a few minutes.

Alright.

Donna continued to roll the chicken pieces that she was planning to fry in bread crumbs, and then set them under the broiler. She steamed asparagus, and then made the hollandaise sauce to pour over it. Donna began to take deep breaths and tried to calm herself down. Her mind began to wonder. I do everything for him, and he's so unappreciative, as she set down plates. Thirty minutes later, Rick finally came downstairs, and sat at the table. She imagined the two of them making passionate love at the kitchen counter top. He wasn't in the mood for small talk, he just wanted to eat and lay down on the couch after dinner. The muscles along his jaw suddenly began to bunch into knots.

Can't we just eat?

He Never Called Again

Sure, but it would be nice to have a conversation, sometimes.

They ate dinner, as Donna continued making idle conversation.

Is it good?

Yeah.

What's the matter?

Nothing!

I'm tired, can't you leave me alone.

Tired from what?

I work hard all week, don't you understand that.

I work too, Rick.

Why are you always so hostile towards me?

I'm not.

You just never shut up, always talking.

Just leave me alone.

Alright, Rick.

Donna suddenly looked uneasy. She began to sigh, "Rick, sometimes I wonder why the hell I put up with you." If it makes you miserable, then don't. Tears began to flow from her eyes. "Look Donna," he said, I really don't want to get into all this right now. He abruptly left the table and went back upstairs. Donna began putting the dishes in the basin and cleaning up the kitchen. It was hour's later in bed that he began to feel in the mood. His tongue was hot and moist when he pulled her lips apart. With just one of his kisses, he made her wet, like a lake, and left her wanting more. A burning desire was building inside her. She wanted him, needed him, suddenly the sensations began to spiral through her. He pulled her close against him and tightened his arms around her, however she felt him holding back something of himself. She clutched at him, inviting him to deepen the kiss. She began putting her hands on his chest, feeling the sleek muscles. She began touching him eagerly, savoring the heat and strength of his firm body. She began to gasp when she felt his teeth on her nipples. She wanted him. Surely it was impossible for any man, even one with a strong will as Rick's, to look at a woman with such a hot, raging need and still remain dispassionate, and distant. Donna felt his hand glide down her leg. She was throbbing, when he dipped his finger into her. She began to shiver. He withdrew his finger very, very slowly and then began again. His thumb was moving higher, she was on fire. She needed to release. A great tension was building inside of her. She couldn't hold out forever. Without a warning she came in a series of short, brief peaks. It wasn't long after that he began to moan and groan and it was all over. She felt the urge to give in to tears afterwards, she felt the emptiness of making love to him, but she didn't. She suddenly felt the hottest flames turn to ashes. Minutes later, without a word he walked across the room to the bathroom to shower. Donna noticed his mood changing; there was no embrace afterwards, no kiss, and no hug. She stared at him while he walked across the room. It felt real, but then it faded, she thought. Donna was so confused that she didn't even want to think about it, she wanted to fall asleep and pretend it never happened.

It wasn't until that gloomy, rainy evening in November, 1990 that he finally came to the reality that his marriage was over. Donna thought he was working late. Rick decided that evening that he would stop at the bar for a quick drink. His intuitive nature felt that something was wrong. He opened the front door and headed straight for the bedroom. When he opened the

He Never Called Again

door he saw Donna and Matthew passionately making love. The image of them together infuriated him. He went into a rage. He wanted to kill her. Both of them. He walked out of the bedroom and left the house in a fury. Like a madman he gets in his car without destination. He didn't know where to go. Confused. He drove around for an hour, and finally went to his parent's house. It was a week later that Rick would walk to Donna's car.

Under his arm is the newspaper he bought earlier, but it was too bulky for its pages. He has one of the revolvers inside of it. He looked for possible onlookers and then reaches his hand into the wheel well. He closes his eyes, and then opens with a sigh of relief when he feels her keys on top of the front tire. He grips them and then hastens off to her door. He then unlocks her door, leaves it ajar an inch and then heads back to her car, but at the same time he sees her, dressed in a t-shirt, spandex shorts and a walkman, rounding the corner, running towards him. He ducks back out of the way onto her porch. He can't think what to do for a moment, but then a thought comes to him. He leans forward, and tosses the keys underhanded towards the wheel of the car. They bounce off of it onto the ground. He rushes back inside of the house, locks the door. Donna approaches the car, and not seeing the keys on the ground next to the tire, she reaches for them where she expects them to be....when she finds that they are not there, she looks down and discovers them next to her foot. She shapes an expression of "they must have fallen off". She picks them up.

Rick sits in the arm chair, the entry way to his left, the couch to his right. On the couch, the book of "Body for Life" is resting open on its face. Rick sits up

He Never Called Again

straight with the gun still wrapped with the newspaper on his lap. He seems to shiver, when she suddenly unlocks the door....

Listening to the sounds of the music coming from her headphones. She enters, not seeing him at first, taking off her headphones, and removing the walkman from her waist. Then she turns. She gasps at the sight of him, dropping her keys and the walkman. What are you doing here??? What do you want? You scared me! She looks down at the keys and sighs, realizing. He slowly opens the newspaper, revealing the gun. Her eyes widen when she sees it. At that precise moment he wanted to shoot her. Kindly sit down, he commanded.

What are you doing, Rick? Where did you…

Calmly he said, sit the hell down.

Donna complied.

Think, Rick. Think about what you are doing, she said.

I have thought about this……….and you know what, I really didn't have to think at all.

It's really a matter of destiny, he said.

It's a matter of sickness.

Rick stood up, putting the newspaper onto the chair, and holding the gun, but not pointing at her. He glances at his watch and checks the time.

We have a long while to wait. Maybe you want to read the book?

Wait for what?

He walks into the kitchen and Donna stood up.

Wait for what?

I told you to sit down.

Rick pours himself a glass of water.

Sit down.

He Never Called Again

Rick drinks the entire glass and fills the glass again, she didn't comply. He walks out of the kitchen, raises the gun to the level of her face. Donna looks at it, and then to the phone on the end table next to the couch.

I'm going to call the police.

Rick begins to laugh.

Really?

Yes. Because I think you are incapable of shooting me.

Just like I really wasn't capable of smacking you.

You just want attention

I wouldn't argue with that. But it's not your attention I want. Sit down I told you.

No.

He points the gun firmly at her, and steps forward.

It's probably not even loaded.

He suddenly flips open the barrel, drops out one of the bullets into his other hand. He shows it to her.

This would pass through your head like a fleeting thought. The thought and then you're gone like that.

Rick puts it back in the barrel, flips it back.

Sit down.

Donna finally sits. Rick goes back to the couch, lifts the paper, and sits down.

Why do we need to wait?

It's none of your business, and if you do what I say, than there won't be any reason for me to use this.

How long do we have to wait?

Until four AM.

Four AM.

Why?

Read. You have your "Body for life" book.

How can I possibly read with a gun pointed at me?

He Never Called Again

He withdraws it, puts it in his lap.

I'm all stressed out...You know, I think if you gave it to me, I would feel much better....I would concentrate more on the book.

Just shut up and read, or perhaps take a nap or something.

Can I take a shower? I really smell from the jogging.

Don't you want a showered hostage?

Rick raises the gun and leans forward. You know, I really hate that tone of voice, Donna.

If I could shoot that tone of voice of yours, I would. I would shoot it five f*****times!

You women are all alike. Talk, Talk.

Read, take a nap, but shut the hell up.

Fear begins to creep into her and she lowers her gaze, leaning back slowly into the couch.

Rick fills another glass of water at the sink in the kitchen and drinks it down.

Donna had been trying to read the book, puts it down, when he returns to sit on the couch.

Why do you keep looking at your watch?

I told you it's none of your business.

Donna is beginning to lose it. It's clearly my damm business, Rick, when you are holding me f**** hostage in my home.

You mean our home.

It's still my home too.

And I don't care if you don't like my tone of voice. And I don't care if you press that gun to my head, and I don't care if you pass a bullet through my head like a fleeting thought. What a stupid metaphor, just like something you would say.

He Never Called Again

Tears began streaming down her face. And how do you expect me to concentrate on reading? This is one of the reasons I'm divorcing you, I knew there was something very strange about you. My female intuition didn't fail me after all. I knew sooner or later your true colors would come out.

Shut Up!

Rick suddenly stands up, and with a tyrant voice screams out shut up or I will put this to your head, and I will pull the trigger, and I won't even blink. I won't even f*** blink, as everything flies out of your head, every bit of everything that has ruined my life..........and brought me here to this moment, you slut.

Rick throws the newspaper aside, drops the gun into the couch, and lunges towards her.

Donna stands up to get away, but he gets to her first, slapping her hard across the face, grabbing her arm, and throwing her face first into the couch, jamming her face into the cushion, his knee on her back. With his other hand, he reaches for a telephone cord that was in his pocket, wraps it around her wrist, ties her hands tightly behind her back. All the while, she screams, sometimes muffled in the cushion, sometimes it sounded full blown and quite loud.

He reaches madly for her 'Body for Life', rips out some of the pages and begins stuffing her mouth.........

SHUT UP! SHUT THE HELL UP!

Rick continues to rip and fill her mouth with the pages of the book.

You slut!!!!!! How could you, bring someone in this house?

He Never Called Again

Donna begins to gag on the paper, choking and spitting it out…

Rick turns her over, facing him, sitting her up. She begins to spit the rest of the paper into his face. He grabs her mouth firmly, squeezes her cheeks together…

Now you behave. You slut! I will stuff all of these pages in your mouth.

Rick releases her, and steps back, and she begins sobbing, falling to her side, and her head on the tattered and torn book.

I didn't do anything wrong. All I did was find someone who loved me. You never loved me. What's so wrong about that? Please don't hurt me.

Please, she pleaded.

Then just cooperate with me. Do your duty. At this precise moment he wanted to have her one last time, he begins to lower his pants and in a matter of minutes it was all over. Make up for your infidelity, you slut.

Rick retrieves the newspaper, goes back to the couch, picks up the gun and sits down.

He takes a few deep breaths, and closes his eyes.

The windows of the house are dark. But then the living room window lights up.

Rick walks away from the light switch on the wall. Donna struggles to sit up, squinting to adjust to the light.

What time is it? She asked.

Rick checks his watch.

It's ten after nine.

I have to go to the bathroom, said Donna

Alright.

Untie me so I can go.

I'm not doing that.

He Never Called Again

Why not?

Because you can't be trusted.

No woman can be trusted.

Then how can I go to the bathroom?

I don't know.

Please, Rick. I really have to go.

Rick goes to her. She snaps back at him, gasping. He leans down, grabs her by the ankle, and takes off her sneakers and socks. He stands her up and leads her directly to the bathroom.

Rick pushes her into the bathtub, takes her shorts down. By now, she is crying again. He takes off her thong. Rick steps back, and draws the curtain.

You said you had to go, so go ahead.

The sound of her urinating as she cries. Rick grabs a handful of toilet paper. When Donna finishes, he draws back the curtain. He begins to look at her, with a cold, blank stare; he reaches down and begins to wipe her. Rick helps her out of the tub, and then reaches back to turn on the water. After a few seconds he turns it off. Rick leads her into the bedroom, turns on the light. He commands her to sit on the bed.

Rick, please. Please Don't.

He begins looking for underwear in her drawer. Goes to her, and slips it on up to her legs.

She begins to sigh in relief. He frantically looks for a skirt in her closet. He starts it up her legs while she sits and then has her stand up to secure it. Rick pushes her back to sit on the bed. He then looks for a pair of shoes in her closet, and puts them on her.

Good, you are finally cooperating with me.

You didn't try to kick me once.

He leads her back into the living room. A few hours later, Rick taps Donna on her shoulder. She

He Never Called Again

awakes, moaning from the pain of lying on the couch with her hands bound behind her back. Rick holds the gun inside the newspaper under his arm.

It's time.

Time......Time for what?

I'm going to kill you.

You slut!

You deserve to die!

Suddenly a thought passes through his mind. His original plan of calling Matthew and waiting for him to come over and killing them both was suddenly torn apart.

I'll go to jail. I can't do this. I'll spend the rest of my life in jail.

He comes to his senses and storms out of the house. It was the first time in his life that he felt helpless. Shocked and betrayed. The feelings of powerlessness and inadequacy began building up. The insecurities he felt. How dare she do this to me? He thought. Life didn't seem fair to him. He believed he actually tried in the marriage. It wasn't his fault, he believed.

Seven years, it was finally over. Rick's ego was hurt. But he felt the pain of financial loss more. He knew that when she filed for divorce, she would still be entitled to half of the property. The fact that he would lose money perturbed him more than the irresponsible failure as a husband. The pettiness of who gets what dish drove him into a frenzy. He didn't want to part with anything that he believed belonged to him. He used the defense mechanism of projection. Everything was Donna's fault. She had the problem. She left him for another man. Rick lacked self-insight. He felt justified. It was Donna that cheated. He was never caught in the act. It was all Donna's fault for his financial loss.

Rick Jankovich wondered, Can even dying be worse than this? He imagined nothing, thinking of her that night that he had the gun. If only I had killed her that night. Rick tried to amalgamate and align all his betrayals. He wanted to be out of her life. He didn't want to deal with her anymore.

It was a year later that the divorce was finally granted. Donna was still going through the motions of being a divorced woman. She continued to date Matthew. She wanted to take it slow, she didn't want to rush the relationship and make another mistake. She felt wounded and hurt. The next six months went by and she began to feel comfortable in the arms of

Matthew. She wanted to make sure that Matthew was really in love with her. Donna wanted him to be faithful, something that she never found in Rick. Donna and Matthew were married in a quiet ceremony, celebrated by a few friends and family members. Her eyes filled with love as she gazed into Matthew's eyes. Matthew reached out and took Donna's arm, folding it firmly against his side. The moment I saw you at the office, I knew that someday, somehow you would be my wife. At last she had found happiness.

Rick felt rejected and betrayed. He released his frustrations in the arms of many women. He was looking for sex, to prove to himself he wasn't a failure. After the divorce decree, the search for women began. He decided to take a few weeks vacation and fly to Rio de Janeiro. It was there that the hunt commenced. He waltzed into a disco called "Help" and began to feed his inflated ego. The women outnumbered the men ten to one. The club was notorious for hot, wild women. Men flocked to the club; they knew there was plenty of easy prey. He knew that his ego would be inflated. There were women everywhere. The women were quite aggressive and liberal. Women at the club would stake men out and grab their asses. So many beautiful women it was mind boggling. Rick knew that he would feel like the center of attention. The women in the club chased the men, he craved adulation and attention. Rick felt like a spokesman for God. A leader of humankind, surrounded by beautiful women enticing him, desiring him. He felt rejuvenated every time he went to the club, he craved the attention.

It was there that he met Tanya Gomes, a seductive, Brazilian beauty with a resume of men that had more mileage than a Ford Falcon. Rick didn't care. He wasn't looking for love or a relationship. He wanted pure, wild sex. After a few drinks she was overtaken by his charming ways. It was later that evening that he persuaded her to join him in his hotel room. She desired him. Tanya also knew that he was from the U.S.A and had a wallet full of money. He brought her back to the hotel. The room was dark; he began his game of slavery. He ordered her to take her clothes off, and then he wanted her to kneel against the bed. When Tanya kneeled, he grabbed his necktie and began tying her hands with soft ties, securing one to each side of the bed. Rick began pulling her arms forward and tying her wrists, so that her derriere stood exposed and he could have a perfect view. He loved the feeling of being in control, she felt helpless. He slowly began walking out of the room, she begins to think what happened, where is he going. He reenters the room and sees that she has moved a bit to the left. Rick became more aroused. He slowly begins to pull down his black thong, and grabs her. He found what he was looking. A great sexual relationship without commitment. The exploration lasted all night. He wanted an open door policy, and Tanya was far away enough not to pressure him. It was the ideal setup. The sexual relationship lasted for a couple of years. Whenever he had the desire for sun and fun he would fly to Rio and meet his needs for sexual gratification. His promiscuous sexual behavior brought a variety of brief, superficial relationships, numerous affairs, and an indiscriminate selection of sexual partners. He had to prove to himself that Donna didn't leave him because he was undesirable. In the evenings, when he returned back to his apartment, he could relax in peace. He didn't have a choice after the divorce; he had to settle for an apartment in his parents building in Brooklyn. There were no questions asked and no wife, or steady girlfriends; no one to make demands on him. He was his own man, independent to come and go.

He kept an ongoing sexual relationship with a local woman that also lasted a few years.

Sandy Martel was a Pollyannaish type, naive woman. Sandy was his next door neighbor, recently separated from her husband. She found salvation in him. Everything was great in the beginning, until she began pressuring him for a serious relationship. She pressured him to live together. He almost did, however she knew that he would only stay for a short period of time. Her husband offered more security so Sandy decided to reconcile her differences and return back with her husband. She knew that Rick didn't want to get so involved; he wanted to keep on moving from

He Never Called Again

one to another. Roaming and being free. Rick had his charming, superficial ways with women, between flying back and forth to Rio and maintaining his local harem. He remained unmoved and cold. He never believed in his followers love, he was always harsh in testing women's feelings. Rick was only concerned with getting what he wanted, when he wanted it… He had no sense of personal boundaries. Rick expressed his masculine presence. He displayed confidence, and that was what attracted the women to him. His pit bull attitude made him a rare commodity. His what you see is what you get attitude combined with his smooth, slick ways was what attracted women.

It was a scorching day in August, in the year of the new millennium when they first glanced at each other in the elevator. Somewhere between the 4th and 6th

floor. They both worked for JQ. Aero Inc. It was later that same day that they first spoke. She didn't know exactly what was happening to her. She felt the magnetism.

Ana Picasso was a 38, divorced mother of two with a Latin, Mediterranean look about her. A vivacious, voluptuous, woman. A certain sex appeal. Her face was full oval with her dark, mysterious eyes that filled with sparkle. Her mouth was sensual and alluring. Her luscious, long dark hair gleamed with shine. She had an aura about her that displayed contentment and self confidence. Ana had a certain charisma about her that attracted men, a star quality about her. She was the public relations manager for the multi billion dollar aircraft charter and leasing company. Her parents were originally from a northern small village in Spain, surrounded by picturesque mountains. Ana was raised

He Never Called Again

in a crumbling neighborhood in Elizabethtown, New Jersey that was full of racial tension, which muggings and gun shots were part of everyday living. A phoenix rising from the ashes she soared as a graduate of the Superior Academy of Languages, in Switzerland. A few years later she returned back to New Jersey to pursue her career.

After minutes of conversing, she felt the heat and passion. The elevator had stopped and at that minute they quickly exchanged emails. I'll send you an email, said Ana. Alright, replied Rick. The emails started very casual. It was about a month later that they began to get hot and sizzling. Ana also loved to observe the cyber world. She knew that she could entice men by logging on with the screen name of "Miss Universe". Men would flock to her because her screen name represented beauty and sex appeal. That same evening she logged on to the computer and began chatting with Dr. Walt Spellman. His profile with picture read a recently separated, good looking anesthesiologist in his forties. She began to email Walt and shortly realized that he was married with five kids. Ana couldn't get involved with a stranger who perhaps was a desperate, deviated sexual pervert. Walt stalked Ana on the computer. He would send instant messages and continue to communicate with Ana. She finally had to tell Walt, that she met someone so he could back off. Walt wanted to know who this man was. Ana began telling him that it was someone who she met at work. He still pursued. He secretly wanted Ana, because she was unobtainable. He silently watched her every move on the computer.

He Never Called Again

Ana became frightened and told Rick about this stalker on the computer. Rick suggested reporting him. Ana took his advice and contacted the online service. It seemed to work. Ana never had contact with him again. Terrified and frightened Ana thanked Rick. She would on occasion see Rick at work and they would converse during lunch. It was about a month later that they began to meet online. They would log in at 400am. They would interact on the computer. In cyber world, they had an online relationship. Rick was special though. She had met him in person first, and then they met on the computer and began an online relationship. It wasn't long that the instant messages began getting hot and personal. Cyber sex eventually turned into phone sex. The fire burning inside of her, felt like it would never go out. It made her breathless. Ana was a master in the game of sex, perhaps even a scholar; her creativity enhanced the steamy, sizzling emails about fantasies of wearing fishnet stockings, black garter belts. The rituals of excitement, pleasures of reinventing role playing, writing erotic scenes and fantasying about living them out aroused him even more. Ana knew that nothing was more exciting than talking sexy to the man you love and having him talk sexy to you. Ana created scripts of exotic talks. She wanted to provoke him with all the smutty phone sex. She loved to hear him moan. She knew the exact words to say. She mastered the sexy adjectives, juicy, big, wet, hard, and throbbing. The stories of being on a train, with her dress falling open wearing her thigh high stockings, and Rick reaching up to touch her derriere. Then his hand sliding up past her stockings onto her fleshy thighs. Then he would begin to fondle her firm, perky breasts. Bam, Rick would come. They would take turns with exotic stories. The changing of positions to Buddha. Ana loved to tease and intrigue him with various scenarios. Intensity, passion, dynamic flames of a sexual cyber relationship had developed. The erotica aspect was phenomenon, enhanced by her creativity and spontaneity. Kama Sutra, Tantra, Ben WA balls all took part in the exploration.

She kept enticing Rick to get together. It was on the bewitching night of ghosts and goblins that they finally interacted in person. Lust and passion had overcome the doubts of getting together. He hesitated at first, with many things to consider sexual harassment, disappoint and disillusion. Eyes and memory, and his driving male desire, he would soon be with her, she thought triumphantly. Whatever his reasons, he wanted her, and she wanted to provoke him. The fantasy had become reality. He was afraid of enjoying it, however he continued to pursue as the hunter. Rick's ego had been hurt before by his ex-significant other. He vowed never to get emotionally close to anyone again. He mastered self control. He was a non committer.

The more time she spent with him the more he kept surprising her. She began realizing that he was a Neo-Nazi, selfish unhappy man.

Ana tried to understand him and bring out the positive sweet qualities in him. Ana believed everyone was capable of change. For the next fourteen months she listened attentively to everything he said in great detail. She began on a rescue mission to try to understand his behavior and reeducate his views on women. She was determined to go to any extremes to persuade him to commit to her. Ana was looking for a friendship first and foremost and then perhaps a serious relationship. Rick made it quite clear that he didn't want her to get serious. Thoughts of a house, and screaming kids and a lawn mower made his skin crawl. Ana assured him that she had no expectations of a long-term commitment. Perhaps she thought in time he would change his mind. The foundation of the building was achieved. They started out as friends. It wasn't long after that he began disclosing all his beliefs and views on relationships and women. Don't trust men, they are only after one thing. They are all dogs, and they have no feelings whatsoever. They are capable of having sex with the wife in the morning and sex with the girlfriend in the afternoon. They are incapable of feeling remorse or guilt, said Rick.

Pigs! Pigs! Ho's! Ho's! With his demented Manson mentality he would say women are all evil. They stem from the time of Adam and Eve. They are only here on this earth to reprocreate. Women are pigs, look at the porn films, how they love a ménage a trios. The calm after the storm of words became even eerier, Ana listened in thrusting silence. She was speechless. I trust no woman, they are all alike. I don't even trust my own Mother. His mother engulfed his well being to such an overbearing extent that his perversity and obnoxious views on women were damaged beyond hope of repair.

He had become a trash bin of his parent's inhibitions. Mood swings were part of his sadistic behavior. The Madonna/prostitute mode was instilled in his mind. The best relationship is the open door policy, where a man can come and go as he pleased. Rick began seeing Ana after work twice a week. The novelty of excitement and exploration. It didn't take Ana very long to realize his behavior patterns. He would have days of total gloom. Days filled with negativity. Loneliness, anger, haunted by a bitter past. So withdrawn, fragile. He would shield his emotional pain by being insensitive and uncaring. His zero state, inner feelings of emptiness. Rick enjoyed fabricating transparent rationalizations. His favorite one he used always was "you've got to be a realist in this world, and a lot of people are foolish appeasers, atheists and commies.

The sexual encounters were always fulfilling. Every pore in her body wanted his presence beside her, but she felt a curious inexplicable understanding that he wanted to watch her too, and that all her movements, deliberate and innocent, were as provocative to him as kissing her, and that her body was as enticing to his eyes as if she was naked, more so because he was required to imagine the exact shape of her breasts, and the satin slide of flesh of her thighs. Yes, she knew that if she touched herself here and there, she would arouse him past all endurance. Somewhere inside her, she wanted to because that would make her unforgettable to him, and she wanted him to keep coming back to her. His eyes moved, devouring her with a hunger to possess; he yearned to taste her and touch her. He wanted to feel every inch of her body. But slowly, and softly, as he watched her fingers flirt with her neck, touching her mouth, sliding down her throat, tempting him. She knew what she was doing, he thought; here was Eve and voluptuous temptation and what would she do next? He waited, watching her. The sensual tension between them thickened unbearably. Ana lifted her left leg upright so she could wing her arms around her knee. The fingers of her left hand settled lightly around her naked ankle, and she twisted forward slightly to get a firmer grip, and then sent him a provocative look. Rick's eyes flared as her fingers gently slid down her feet to her toes and back to her ankle, and she saw it.

Rick would never forget the picture of her sensual eyes, her body inviting him, and her enticing movements that revealed everything, and nothing. It took just one movement, the knowing elusive smile, and her fingers sliding, and he was ready. She felt as if her body was going to explode as his tongue slicked wetly all over her lips. He pulled her up to him so she could feel his huge pulsating length, and her arms were around his neck. His hand moved as he lifted her buttocks, and he held her there, his fingers digging into the lush flesh, thrusting her tighter and tighter against his erection. Ana felt his rock-hard manhood and his hands caressing her body everywhere he could reach, and he felt her everywhere, between her legs, her thighs, her buttocks, and her pencil eraser nipples. Rick wanted her, and she wanted him too.

Don't stop....With her pouty lips, Ana enticed him more. He kissed her tongue, lips, and breasts. He parted her lips more fully; he teased them with his fingers and his tongue, exploring her with his lips and fingers deep within the sensitive recesses. It was the taste of her, those luscious lips that excited him.

Ana, he moaned.

She licked it.

She groaned and he kissed her lips. You'll have to stop kissing me

I can kiss something else.

Ana made a little sound in the back of her throat, a sound of excitement, invitation.

He Never Called Again

What will you kiss that will feel as good as this? Or taste so good? She whispered in his ear. Ana reached for him again, enticing him with her sensual movements against his body. Rick wanted her body now. He needed her, he wanted her. He saw it in her eyes that erotic light flared in his response, like a Roman candle. He began cupping her breasts. You're beautiful, he whispered, sliding his hands over her body.

Kiss me, she murmured, loving him for saying that, maybe he meant it, but she wouldn't stop to think of it.

Rick had to excel in something, so he put all his creative energies in sex. Ana knew that Rick was the only man who satisfied her. She became obsessed with him, shopping for black thongs, garter belts, toys. Hundreds of dollars were spent on her hair, makeup and clothes, so she would look perfect for him. She dieted and exersized to keep in shape for him. Ana always dressed seductively hot for him. She knew he was the only man who matched her intensity and sexual drive. The ultimate lover. Sexually no one would ever hold a candle to him.

Rick's life was unfulfilled. He was a man who blamed everyone for his problems. Rick was a classic version of a narcissist. Incapable of loving anyone but himself.

Ana was soon approaching her 39th birthday. Her strategy was to ask him to spend a weekend together. Quality time, to get him a little closer to her. She asked her Mom if she could watch the kids for the weekend. Her son Paul was fifteen and her daughter Tammy was seven. It was still the honeymoon stages of the relationship, so he complied.

It was a beautiful Indian summer day in November that they met at the usual numbered spot at the parking lot of JQ Aero Inc. He was carrying a dozen long stemmed American beauty roses. How romantic, Ana thought. Happy Birthday! Thank you! That was so sweet of you.

They passionately kissed for a minute. He strutted back to his car and locked it up, and took the drivers seat in Ana's car.

Where are we going?

I don't know.

Do you want to go for a drive?

It's such a beautiful day, let's take a drive to Point Pleasant beach, replied Ana. The forty five minute drive on the Garden State Parkway seemed forever. She wanted him, desired him. Ana began sliding her hand up and down his pants. Slowly reaching for the bulge. The thrust of desire was overwhelming her. The first stop after exit 98 was to the liquor store to pick up one of the finest, sparkling bottle of champagne. Ana began to notice his mood changing when his frugal mind began calculating the price. Hotel room, liquor, this is costing me a fortune, he thought. He was still in the excitement stages. The impressive beginnings. The predator after his prey.

The search for a room ended with a musty filled nautical room overlooking the ocean. Walking from the car to the hotel entrance filled Ana full of adrenaline. It seemed forever. Rick drew her inside and laid her down on the huge bed. The weekend was spent in bed with the experimenting of the Buddha positions, filled with strawberry body creams, Dolphins Tickler, Roman candles, and the ten inch dildo. Ana was a wild tigress with a few sips of the bubbly. Her imagination ran wild with her. She slowly reached for the Ben WA balls that were placed on the dresser table and started heading for the backdoor. At first Rick hesitated, but then he loved the excitement of something new and thrilling. It was that same evening that she performed the shaving ritual with his Norelco shaver. Rick followed her to the bathroom. Gazing at the mirror, she was behind him, her right hand on his chest. She continued shaving every bit of hair on his body. He was so manly with a Greek Adonis body. His body was perfectly sculpted. She loved his physique. After the duck's bill and wibbling, her body was full of oil; she wanted to feel the exhilarating sensation of water, a soothing sensual shower. The fantasy of both showering together became real. Ana turned the knob and the seduction of the water dripping on there faces stimulated her more. While in the shower she began telling him an erotic fantasy. It was to cold to go to the beach, so she began fantasizing with her sultry, sexy voice she began saying, as you were lying on your beach towel on the sand, I see you from a distance. I'm watching you from afar. You begin rubbing the oil on your body in the hot sun. I slowly walk towards you and I provocatively, take off my white top and skirt, and drop it close to you on your towel, wearing only my bikini bottom. I go into the ocean. You pretend to be sleeping when I begin splashing droplets of water on your face. I slowly knee next to you with my long, dark, damp hair, caressing your hot burning body. I softly begin licking your lips, and earlobes. You are lying there in silent yet becoming very aroused. That was the prelude for another round of sessions. They managed to get dressed and walked downstairs to the car. Rick was famished and stopped at the first

He Never Called Again

restaurant he saw. Sitting at the table, Ana slowly began to slip her right shoe off and head for the hills.

Stop, he shouted.

No one is looking, replied Ana.

She began to see a change in him. Within a few minutes the waitress came over with the menus. He selected the meatloaf. It was at that time his mind wandered for a moment and he began remembering of the time he was growing up. They would live on pork and beans everyday and his Mother would only cook meatloaf only on Sundays. Ana ordered the deluxe cheeseburger. Ana couldn't believe the way he divulged his dinner in a matter of seconds. It was like watching someone indignant on a rampage. Suddenly she began to hear a strange sound coming out of his mouth. What is he doing? she thought. He was sucking on his teeth. Rick twisted the toothpick dispenser, which was fully stocked with picks. The cool feel of the wood against his teeth, he began picking on his teeth, with his left index finger he reached for his mouth and slowly began dissecting the food particles from his teeth. Oh God, how gross, Ana thought. Imagine him at Tavern on the Green, doing that, she thought. They headed back for the room and were ready for another round of sessions. The sex was so mesmerizing, so intense. In the darkness of the night she inserted her finger in the back door with the help of Ky jelly. Ana expressed all his desires with hands and fingers. Ana became obsessed with pleasing him. She wanted to break all Guinness world records of figure eights and lollipop licking. She loved to flick her tongue backward and forwards. She knew how to use her tongue with the same technique of twanging a guitar string. Then she began humming with the

He Never Called Again

magical ring that she placed on him. It vibrated his colossal copulatory organ. Then she used her secret technique. She placed her wet hand around the shaft and started all over again. She was a real boundary-breaker with the toys. The next morning was another round of sessions, he began to withdraw and panic the Ben WA balls were not coming out. Driving back home she slowly began teasing him by lifting her skirt and the sight of self touching aroused him. Rick loved watching the way she slid her fingers inside. He was so aroused. He loved driving while Ana fondled him. The drive from the beach was a few hours longer than usual. They stopped in the secluded rest area off of the parkway and began the adventures in the woods. The earthy open air turned him on even more. The evening was parted with a prolonged, wet kiss. It seemed to Ana that they were getting closer than they had ever been. She always felt she never knew when he would call her again. She felt the emptiness of uncertainty. Ana was blinded by the obsession of love and sex. The animal magnetism. The red flags she overlooked. The painful unique sign of a non committal man. He always left her with an uncomfortable feeling of things left up in the air.

Wondering?

Would he call again?

When would he call? Ana began analyzing his behavior pattern.

What did I do?

Was it something I said?

Ana begin thinking why he was so afraid of getting involved. Rick found so many excuses why he couldn't get serious. He was so evasive with his Houdini-like ability to escape any questions. Ana never asked

He Never Called Again

questions she knew that if she began cross-examing him he would run. She had to maintain a certain non interested, I don't care attitude with him. As soon as he sensed she was getting to close he would run to his cave. He was the conqueror he was only interested in the chase. The monogamous relationship was boring to him. The subject of marriage would come up and then he would punish her by not calling for a few days. The 400am phones calls slowly began diminishing. Ana loved to hear his voice early in the morning he had a certain sexy way about him that the sound of his voice instantly made her climax.

The survival of the test of time was questioned when in the end of November, he was sent on a business trip to Hawaii. It's only going to be a few weeks, said Rick. Before you know it I'll be back. I'll miss you, said Ana. Stop, he said. Stop the Bullshit.

The days were filled with business meetings, the nights filled with women. It didn't take long for Rick to unravel his true colors, his core of deception.

She was the lady of the night that paced the hotels looking for clients. She particularly liked the Japanese clients. She was the typical, unscrupulous prostitute. Marina lacked mystique and class. The sun was still shining when the meeting was over at 5 and that late afternoon as Rick was chatting with his co workers in front of the hotel. His wandering eyes noticed the long black hair to her waist, the double d's busting out of her t-shirt and the tight purple spandex mini skirt. That was enough for him to become interested and aroused. The glib, superficial charm effortlessly erupted.

You are gorgeous.

Are you staying at the hotel?

No, but I can be, she said. He knew right away what she was aiming for.

You must be from Brooklyn?

Why?

It's you accent.

I'm from Brooklyn too.

He knew that it would cost him. So his ploy, was to think of a way that he didn't have to pay for services. You know I'm going to be here for a few weeks with my buddies, perhaps we can make a deal.

What do you have in mind? I'll get you three guys and the deal is you won't charge me. Alright, she said.

What's your name, asked Rick.

Marina! Flashing her business card, he quickly accepted without hesitation.

The very next day Rick looked at her flashy business card with her huge tits piercing out and dialed her number. The deal was set up. Marina was originally from Greece, but moved to Maui to solicit her services. She loved the exotic weather. Sun filled days and nights of lying on her back. The easy life for the non ambitious.

She knocked at the hotel door at midnight, after her other appointments were met. Marina began telling Rick, about the business of tax free cash. She actually enjoyed the fact that her illicit business brought in enough money that she could afford a new jaguar. Rick enjoyed listening to the juicy tales of her quickies. He felt comfortable with Marina, since she wasn't looking for a serious relationship. It was pure sex, no feelings or emotions. Rick feared attachment and was incapable of love. Marina had no feelings for men, they were all the same. Rick found a safety net without attachment for four weeks.

Rick finally called Ana a couple of days before he left Maui. Arriving at the airport testing the waters he called Ana to let her know that he just flew in. Ana was so deeply in love with Rick that she welcomed him back home with open arms. Ana never questioned him that he only called her once in four weeks. She wanted to see him, it had been four weeks. She really missed him. Rick called a week later and they began just where they left off. He came back sporting a beautiful deep dark tan. The sensual wet kisses melted her. It was magical just like the beginning of the romance. He pacified Ana with a few souvenirs, making her think that he missed her and was thinking of her. The setting of the encounters was almost always in the car. It was the classic, going all the way sex game of the 1940's. Rick was the back seat lover tearing off Ana's bra with his teeth. The session was extremely hot, since it was four weeks that he was gone and she missed him terribly.

The Christmas holidays were soon approaching and he was hesitant in seeing Ana. She began to wonder why? She knew that he was frugal, but how she wondered could he be so cruel not to see her for Christmas. She began thinking perhaps he didn't have time to buy her a gift. She tried to make him feel comfortable. I didn't buy you a Christmas present, the only present I have for you is me, she said. Rick felt better; he didn't want to be pressured. He spent over a thousand dollars in Hawaii the month before. He was a taker not a giver.

He Never Called Again

Alright, I'll meet you at 4, he said.

The anticipation of another round of sessions, Ana thought. It's been four long weeks, he should sound a little more excited to see me, she thought.

Christmas Day was celebrated in the park surrounded by scenic views of snow covered trees overlooking the ice filled lake. Capturing the moment the poloraid camera was used as a prop. Ana began pouring Champagne and the drops of what were left were poured down her thighs. The slipping and sliding of the bottle captured the effect of the infamous picture.

Hold it!

Perfect!

Slide it in again. The many poses with the bottle excited him more. The sweat poured down his forehead and face dripping on her firm, large breasts. Now he had pictures of her, incriminating pictures. Ana trusted him. Together they had found ecstasy. Ana was brilliant in her games. She especially loved the sexual banquet. Ana smothered Rick with whipped cream, crushed fruit and custard. She loved stimulating his appetite. She began by slowly dripping honey into his belly button, then taking an orange and squeezing it onto his skin, and then pouring chocolate sauce as the final ingredient. Ana made Rick her plate which the food was served, and she was the only diner. The once a week sessions continued routinely. Ana thought she found a special man, a soul mate.

Rick encouraged her with his passion and lust. He knew that there was no one in the world who would love him unconditionally as her. He was afraid, incapable of giving or receiving love. It was a few days before the traditional day of Lovers, and the weekly car session was planned with a private celebration. Ana wanted to celebrate on a sheepskin rug in front of a roaring log fire but Rick was content on driving to a secluded parking place.

I have to stop at the store.

No problem.

Driving passed the seven eleven he realizes that it would be a good idea if he buys her a present. After all it was Valentine's Day, he thought. Wait here in the car, he commanded.

Alright!

I'll be right back. Ana's face dropped when he walked back to the car, and opened the bag and gave her a Teddy Bear, it said I love you. Ana grabbed the teddy bear that said I love you with a heart shaped red satin bow, and reached out to kiss him passionately. Rick immediately said, don't get too excited.

Why?

The bear said I love you, not me.

But I love you, Rick

What?

I can't believe you said the L word.

Yes, I did.

I really love you.

No you don't.

What is Love, he asked.

Love is……

Love is……

Love is a package.

Filled with Trust, Caring, Sharing, Lust, Passion, Understanding, Unconditional Love.

He Never Called Again

Ana was waiting for some response on his part, perhaps I love you too, but there was nothing from him, just a moment of silence.

Ana twirled the teddy bear around by one of his stubby arms. Ana was confused. He realized after giving her the teddy bear that she was getting closer to him. Rick maintained evasive and aloof for the next few weeks. The inward struggle between his feelings were driving him crazy. He wanted and desired Ana, he groaned with delight whenever he thought about how she twanged his guitar. Enraged and afraid, he had to manage somehow to preserve his self control. A perfect game of punishment and reward. Rick's journey was to keep her confused. He wanted her, just for easy, convenient sex.

Rick didn't care about her feelings at all. Rick began to feel that she was getting to close to him. He suddenly realized everything that he had done had been far more effective than he could ever imagine. Everything was working far too well. Suddenly he was beginning to panic. He found himself thinking things like, "Don't do this……..there are so many other women out there. They continued to see each other on and off. They were like two planets in orbit, sometimes close but never completely in each other's world.

The birds were chirping early in the morning that spring day in May as he was walking towards his car. Without any apparent reason he began feeling an excruciating pain, an electric shock as he struggled to get in his car. The pain and agony he felt made him stop the car and he managed to turn back around and go home. He had the stuck in the middle apartment in his parent's commercial building. Walking sideways

He Never Called Again

he managed to open the door. He couldn't walk. He began to crawl up the stairs. He managed to get inside the door of his bedroom, and he laid on his bed. The pain was intensifying. He began to cry. The sharp pain felt like a knife poking through his skin. Such agonizing pain that it was indescribable. His face full of agony and pain. Oh God what is happening to me, he silently grunted. He yelled out for his Mother.

Call the doctor, Mom.

Why?

What's wrong?

I don't know, I can't move …….I'm in so much pain.

Mrs. Yankovich called the doctor and managed to schedule an appointment for that very afternoon. Barely walking to the car, he sat sideways in the passenger's seat. Restlessly, he waited for his name to be called. Thank God, I 'm next, he thought. The pain was intensifying. He slowly walks inside the doctor's office feeling like an 80 year old man. He managed to sit in the chair; his face seemed to have lost some color.

Hello, said Dr. Goldman.

Hello, Doctor I'm in so much pain, I could barely walk.

I don't know what's happening to me.

The doctor commands him to the examining room. Where does it hurt Rick?

It's my back I don't know what happened. I can't seem to straighten up.

You will have to lay here on the tabie, said Doctor Goldman.

Can you manage?

Struggling he managed to lie down on the examining table. Did you fall?

No, Doctor, all of a sudden I just couldn't walk and the pain began shooting down my right leg. He struggled to take off his shirt, the pain was unbearable. The doctor began feeling his back and said the symptoms are those of a herniated disk. I'm going to give you a prescription for an anti inflammatory, a sedative and I'm going to recommend you see a Chiropractor. Take this medication once a day and make an appointment for the chiropractor as soon as you can. I'll see you in my office in a week. Thank you Doctor, said Rick. You should feel a little better once you take the Viaox.

Unshaven, he managed to put his shirt on, and walk through the doctor's waiting room without looking up at anyone. His mother took the wheel of the car and the ride home seemed forever. She dropped him at home and drove to the pharmacy to fill his prescription. Rick's pain of expression on his face deepened. He was concerned. What is happening to me, he thought. The baby steps that he took climbing the stairs back to his room seemed forever. His mother managed to fill the prescription in less than an hour. His mother handed him a glass of water and the prescriptions that were still sealed in the paper bag. He tore off as quickly as he could the prescriptions from the bag and swallowed the sedative first and then the Viaox. The pain was still excruciating.

He wanted to be alone with his pain and agony. Call me if you need anything Rick, said his Mother.

Yeah, said Rick.

The pills were beginning to take effect and suddenly he feels his eyelids drooping. Waking up in the middle of the night, the worst nightmare of his life. The pain is still there. Wondering. What the hell is going on with me, he logs on to the computer and begins researching herniated disk problem. A quick overview of the spine begins to shine some light on him. Searching the internet he learns that when a disk is herniated, the surrounding tissue becomes swollen and inflamed. The tissues and the disk press against the spinal nerve therefore resulting in pain, and numbness. Rick leaned back in severe pain and agony to glare at the computer screen. That's exactly what it is. Scared and terrified, his heart is racing. He couldn't feel his toes they were numb. The sharp pain was radiating from his back down through the leg onto his foot. It was Sciatica. It was the pressure on the spinal cord affecting the ability of the nerves to send messages from the brain to the systems of the body that control the sensory, motor, and autonomic function.

Oh My God, he thought. The very next day he had the appointment to see Dr. Silver; he was the chiropractor that his family doctor recommended. After using a number of different tests in the examination Dr. Silver determined that in fact it was a herniated disk, L5, L7.

Rick I have some bad news for you, if your condition does not improve within a few weeks it is strongly recommended that you have back surgery. Let's try the conservative method first. We'll get you into therapy and see how that works, and how you feel, said Dr. Silver. Alright, but the pain is still excruciating, said Rick. He leaned toward the desk and felt that he was losing control of his life. He had called out sick from work, and Ana was beginning to wonder

He Never Called Again

why he hadn't called her. It was over a week, she was quite concerned. She felt something, her intuition just knew, she felt something was wrong. What could it be? Ana began thinking he is being an asshole. Why isn't he calling me? She began analyzing what she did, or said that had perturbed him. She finally couldn't take it any more and called him at home. His mother picked up the phone.

Hello!

May I speak to Rick?

He's sleeping, she said.

I was concerned about him that's why I'm calling, said Ana.

He's sick, it's his back. What happened? said Ana I don't know his back just starting hurting him. Ana inquired about him. She began telling his Mother how concerned she was and hoped he felt better. The next day Rick finally called, his voice had a sadness overtone and he began expressing his concern about his health. Weeks went by and the pain was still intense, his sister Martine who was a registered nurse suggested a neurosurgeon, a specialist. It was a week later that his appointment with Dr.Berdick, left him discombobulated. The evaluation confirmed that in fact his herniated disk was severely damaged. The series of x-rays and magnetic resonance imaging scans all confirmed the dreaded reality that in fact the operation was necessary. Rick's severe episode of pain was depressing him. The surgical procedure was known as microdiskectomy, it involved the open removal of the part of the herniated disk that put pressure on the spinal cord.

Rick was terrified. It was a major operation requiring general anesthesia, the dissection of muscle, removal of bone, and a possible bone fusion. Weeks of pain and suffering were soon to be diminished. Ana was so frightened and concerned that she also researched the surgical treatment of the herniated disk.

The day was rainy and gloomy. Rain pounded against the 4th floor window of the hospital bed. Rick's heart felt dead, he wanted to cry. He glanced at the room that was nicely wallpapered. His arm was connected with a plastic tube, the intravenous bag was mounted. He couldn't feel his toes, they were numb. He looked drained and scared. He felt a transition to another level of awareness, the moving of a flesh body into another. The operation was scheduled for the morning, his mind wandered, he is scared.

What if I die? Rick thought.

The entourage of support would be there waiting for him when he returned. Rick's parents and sisters were all concerned. Ana had a sullen look of concern. The nurse walks in the room smiling and tries to cheer him up. She slowly begins to roll the hospital bed to the elevator up to the 6th floor where the operating room was scheduled for him. Rick begins to make idle conversation with her, as she tries to reassure him he'll be alright. How long is this operation? It's a few hours, she responded. You'll be alright! It will be over before you know it.

How are you feeling? said, Dr Berdick.

Nervous? You'll be under general anesthesia.

Dr. Walt Spellman, will be with you in a few minutes to ask you a few questions. I'll see you in fifteen minutes. Hello, I'm Dr. Walt Spellman; I need to ask you a few questions. First you need to fill out

He Never Called Again

this questionnaire and I'll be back in five minutes. Dr. Spellman reenters the room and after looking over the form has an incredulous look on his face. He was tall, blond and very handsome, his hair was picture perfect. It can't be him, Dr Spellman, thought. Is it Rick? All those months of trying to find out who Rick was, he is right here in front of me, at my mercy. I despise him. I must be professional, he silently thought, this means that Ana must be here in the hospital too. I still love her, why can't I get her out of my mind.

Rick, I'm going to give you morphine through the intravenous bottle and you'll be out in less than five minutes, said Dr. Spellman.

A state of confusion rushes through Dr. Spellman mind, he's tempted to get him out of the way. What if I get caught? There is no way, I'm too clever. They will never figure it out. I'll have to somehow manage to get the nurse out of the room. He began to plot. I've got it, instead of 2-5/10 micrograms. I'll double the amount.

Nurse can you hand me, another bag of intravenous from the room next door.

Alright, I'll be right back.

While she's gone he slips the liquid in.

They will never know.

The operation was completed. Rick is surrounded by the doctor and nurses overlooking his vital signs in the recovery room. His blood pressure begins to drop. His breathing pattern changes, his eye movements. A state of emergence. A state of delirium. He slips into a coma.

Dr. Berdick walks downs to the room. His voice sounded shaky and forlorn. I'm sorry but Rick slipped into a coma. What? shouted his Mother. I'm not going to lie to you, it looks very serious. Is he going to make it? I don't know, he's unconscious. Overcome by shock and disbelief his parents and sisters look distraught. Ana is in a state of shock and disbelief.

Doctor, What happened?

Can we see him? said Mrs. Yankovich.

He needs to stay in the intensive care unit for the next few hours.

We need to monitor him.

I'll be back as soon as I can.

Dr. Berdick returned in an hour. I'm sorry he's still in a coma, nothing has changed. Ana's face was flushed with tears falling down her face. Ana couldn't believe she was losing Rick. The night seemed forever, she stayed at the hospital waiting for some sign of hope. The visiting hour was over. The nightmare of the ordeal was mind boggling. Ana wanted to stay, but her kids were at home waiting. Ana reached for her cell phone in her bag and called her Mom. She begged and pleaded for her Mom to watch them a little longer. She couldn't leave Rick there in the hospital so helpless. Rick's parents and sisters looked haggard. I think we'll go home for a while to rest and we'll come back in a while, said Mrs. Yankovich. I'll stay here until you get back, said Ana. A few moments later, Dr. Spellman walks in the room. Preparing herself, she took a deep breath. Ana felt something was terribly wrong. When she looked up and saw who it was, he smiled. He looked familiar but where do I know him from, she thought.

Who are you?

I'm Dr. Walt Spellman.

Ana walked closer to him, and started to shake. She tried to remain composed, but she was frightened.

What happened to Rick?

He Never Called Again

Is he going to be alright?

Oh My God!

Ana tries to remember, he looks familiar, but she doesn't remember where she knows him from.

Are you the Doctor, she asked?

Yes I'm a doctor, but I'm the anesthesiologist.

I was Rick's anesthesiologist.

Ana's mouth was painfully dry. For a moment she couldn't speak and stared right into his eyes.

How is he doing?

He's still the same, he said.

I can't believe she doesn't remember me, he thought. He paused, a bitter expression on his face. If I tell her who I am, she'll suspect something. I'll lose my medical license; I'll be arrested for attempted murder. I better leave, he thought.

He'll be fine, I'm sure, he said.

Ana took another look at him, but she just couldn't remember, he looked so familiar, she thought. Good night, I'll stop by tomorrow morning, he said breaking the short silence.

The very next morning, Dr. Spellman continued checking on his patients in the East wing of the hospital.

The following day the question still hovered on her mind. Where did I know that Doctor from?

Ana was back at the hospital in the afternoon, and finally Rick was out of the intensive care unit. The smell of the red roses, as she walked in the room almost brought tears to her eyes. She remembered the time he gave her flowers on her birthday. He still had no idea she was there. She began talking to him, but he was in another world. Weeks went by, and he still hadn't regained consciousness.

He Never Called Again

The sunlight streaming through the hospital window touched her face. Ana suddenly closed her eyes and fantazised that he was alright. She began to pray for a miracle.

Ana glanced over to Rick and his eyes suddenly begin to blink, then slowly his eyes opened fully. Ana couldn't believe the miracle that was happening before her. She runs out of the room and calls the nurse. Ana began thanking God, silently. The nurse calls for the Doctor, and he comes in to examine him. He's going to be alright!, said Dr. Berdick.

Thank God, said Ana.

He won't remember anything, but he'll be fine.

He'll need a few months of therapy for his back, but the worse is over.

That about covers it, it certainly was a close call.

This is a real miracle, responded Ana.

It was a slow process but Rick was on his way to recovery. The following months were taken very easy with lots of rest and relaxation. He was almost eighty percent better. Lonely and horny, he picked up the phone and dialed Ana. It had been a few months since he had his sexual needs filled. Rick desired Ana, he needed sex.

Rick began seeing Ana again on a weekly basis, it didn't take him long to revert to his behavior pattern. He always left her hanging, not knowing when he would see her again, or call. If she didn't love him so much, she would have given up. She loved him unconditional. She wasn't interested in another relationship. She just wanted Rick. The feeling of loneness and uncertainty whenever he left her, made her feel sad and empty. She could have any man she desired. Why, she wondered was she so obsessed with him. Was it that he was the only man that satisfied her? Was it because he was a challenge? Why couldn't he commit? What was he afraid of? Something wasn't right. She felt empty. Lonely, whenever he wasn't around. She didn't like the way he made her feel. Sex. Was this only about sex? Didn't he care? Ana couldn't control her feelings. She was emotional, even though she always told Rick that she was unemotional. She thought of him as her hero, her knight in shining armor. She tried to stop her emotional feelings and treat him just like a piece of ass too. It was hard. Ana was in love with him. She thought of him at unexpected times, throughout the day and night. Looking back she remembered the time they made passionate love at work. The thrill, the excitement, the risk of being caught. The imagined risk that heightened the sexual encounter, raising adrenaline levels. They met in the bathroom, in the pilot's shower room, the water running in the shower, thoughts of his tongue pressing its way between her teeth, biting her lips, the throbbing heat of the two bodies, the sexual arousal, the thrust, moving harder and harder. The two bodies embracing the complications of an incredible erotic experience. It was that same night that he had a dream, or a nightmare, he thought. It was so real to him, so frightening. He dreamt that he was at his own wedding again. The room was gigantic and foreboding, with huge doors made of steel. No sooner did his dream begin that he found himself taking vows. When it was his turn to say, "I do," he was overcome by panic. He wanted to run out but he couldn't because he allowed it to go too far. He had no choice so he said, "I do." He saw Ana in his dream, wearing a beautiful white beaded elegant wedding dress, imagined her wearing

He Never Called Again

her white thigh highs and garter belt. The second those words were out of his mouth he felt sick. He thought, "How could I have done this? My life is over." Rick's fear was so real and so profound that it startled him out of his sleep. When he woke up he still felt the terror, but he was also angry at Ana in the dream for making him experience those awful feelings. It was after that dream that whenever he reached for the phone to call her, he would get a sinking feeling in the pit of his stomach. Somehow he resented Ana for that dream. His fear of phoning her became greater. He didn't want to run into her at work, he was nervous and afraid. He told himself that he didn't want to confront any anger she might be harboring because he hadn't called. He told himself that she would argue with him, so he did everything he could to avoid talking to her, remaining distant and aloof. How could he explain to her what he was feeling? He couldn't understand it himself. All he knew was that he wanted to get as far away from her as he possibly could. What they shared, hot and volatile as it been, wasn't just sex. He recognized that. He just wasn't prepared to face the truth. Love didn't enter into this, even if he wanted it to. Who the hell am I kidding, he thought. What they shared had been some of the best moments of his life, not to mention the best sex, of his life.

Rick was confused, he was torn. Somewhere deep inside he did love her in his way, he did care about her. Rick wanted to express his tender emotions, but somehow he didn't know how, on the other hand, he was experiencing fear, anxiety and panic. All the feelings that made Rick run.

Rick was attracted to Ana, and he liked her. Deep inside of him he admired Ana, for her competence and

He Never Called Again

intelligence. He just didn't know why he treated her so badly. Perhaps it was his internal alarm system that he thought he had to put out the fire.

It was in the horrifying month in September, with the loss of five thousand souls when Ana had Rick on her mind, she just couldn't stop thinking of him. She was driving on the New Jersey Turnpike in her black explorer, with the tractor trailers flying by, turning up the volume to the sounds of "Bon Jovi's, Runaway Girl" she remembered when the Suv began to rollover. Suddenly it felt like she had been thrown out of the universe. She could hear noises, and see the figures in the distance. They seemed to be wearing white robes, and they were faceless. They were in torment. They were helpless and gesturing her to join them. Then in fear she realized it would be like that forever.

Rose F. Quintiliano

Something was happening; she didn't know what it was. They were sending her a message, something about making a choice. They were talking to her. Ana was shown through a tunnel of events that were likely to happen in the near future. Ana was made to understand that nothing is absolutely fixed and that everything depends on how one chooses to use free will; even if the events are predestined it could be changed or modified by a change in the way one relates to them. The voices saying that the future of great environmental destruction will lead to the establishment of the environmental religion. The ultimate collapse of the World economy. The visions of the glowing ball of flame in the destruction of Rome, Italy and the Vatican. The terrifying scenes of a terrible war between China and Russia. The futuristic society that is required to have a computer chip implanted in the bodies containing an individual's personal information. The sights of the rest of the people who refused to have the chip implanted would then be considered the so called outcasts. The voices saying if humanity changed for the better, a horrible world war would be averted through spirituality instead of materialism.

The visions of natural disasters that caused famine and starvation, the increase of hurricanes and floods and earthquakes and volcanoes. Eventually the world will become more peaceful, the natural disasters will end and a greater spirituality will come to humanity. The visions of the shift of the earth's axis resulted in massive earthquakes and tidal waves. The voices saying that the conversion of China to God will be seen as a way to prevent global war.

Rose F. Quintiliano

The war between the forces of light and the forces of darkness growed so intense on earth, humanity was seen as a danger of being consumed by the forces of darkness. The vision of the slipping of Japan into the ocean. How terrifying. The voices saying that there will be three days of darkness for the explosion of volcanoes. Humanity will always have the light. The vision of the government falling down. The sounds of the faceless screaming out America will not be completely destroyed, she listened attentively. The powerful words saying, the world will experience tremendous upheavals. Ana's Suv then flipped over.

The voices saying that the great suffering will occur because humans are breaking the rules of the universe. Humanity is being consumed by the cancers of arrogance, materialism, racism, chauvinism and separatist thinking. There will be a cleansing of the

He Never Called Again

earth will result for the purpose of education. The voices were getting louder saying that humanity will become born again. It will be a long, painful process, but humanity will emerge humbled, educated, peaceful, and unified. The explorer stopped flipping.

Was this a dream? Am I dreaming this, she thought? Suddenly, she didn't know anymore, she couldn't understand it. Ana felt like her body had floated up to the ceiling. The dust on top of the light fixtures. The doctor examing her on the table, she suddenly realized it was her, it was her body. Ana saw her family waiting in the hall, she saw her kids crying uncontrollably. She wanted to tell them to please stop crying. She wanted to tell them she was fine, however they didn't hear her. She was alright. Ana wanted to get back to them in a hurry, she wanted to watch them grow up.

Suddenly her eyes slowly began to open in the emergency room. She didn't understand what had happened. Ana walked out of the emergency room a few hours later with only a few minor bruises to her leg. She felt something different about her, but it was totally unexplainable. What had happened? Her mind was wondering from mixtures of confusion and disbelief. Ana felt disoriented.

It was sometime a month later. Ana began unlocking Rick's past with a massive cast iron skeleton key. Ana began to realize he was the one with problems. It was his insecurities, his blocked wall. He didn't want a relationship. She began thinking was it only with me, he didn't want a relationship. Or anyone? Ana came to the realization she could not change him. It didn't matter to her anymore. Ana had given up all hope. The tactics she tried were to no

He Never Called Again

avail. She even tried the so called rules. The rules of acting indifferent, aloof. Being busy and unavailable. Being unobtainable. Ana had to do a 360 degree turn. The 35 rules of manipulation and masquerade. The extra rules of silently counting to five before saying yes to go out with him.

Rick and Ana connected in a way that went beyond romance, beyond friendship, beyond what ever they had before. She thought he was special, and had found her soul mate. She couldn't explain it. Ana felt the romance had defied time, distance and changes within them. Ana's spirit lifted whenever she spoke to him. The sound of his sexy voice always turned her on, and made her melt with passion. Whatever anger she felt subsided when she heard his sexy, charming voice. She felt it was a once in a lifetime connection. She wanted to use sex as a tool. She wanted to live happily ever after. Ana was no different than any other woman, she wanted love. She desperately tried to keep her man by working hard at being the most giving, lovable woman in his life. She overwhelmed him with love letters, emails, and love poems. Ana gave him advice; she lavished Rick with praise, sexual attention, affection. She made him feel like the most loved man in the universe. She wanted him to love her. Ana was also in love with his potential. She thought she could change him.

He never once said I love you. She filled all the emotional blanks. Sometimes Ana felt like she was rowing the boat alone. Ana worked hard for his love.

It was the end of December, a crisp bitter day that she finally realized that he wasn't giving back the same emotional love. He hadn't called in over a month. She wanted to talk to him; she called him early in the day. He was ignoring her phone calls. Lonely and desperate, she called again. She began confiding in her best friends, Debbie Stevens and Lucinda Girt.

Debbie was her confidant, her tower of hope, she turned to Debbie for advice, and support. At times Ana felt she was losing her mind. She was her rock of Gibraltar. Debbie encouraged her, gave her strength to go forward. Debbie was a petite, slender woman, in her late thirties, with a beautiful tanned flawless skin. She was married for over a decade and knew what made men tick.

Lucinda was her other confidant, who also gave her moral support. Lucinda was also in her late thirties, tall and well-proportioned. Her hazel-green eyes shined with radiance. She was a divorced mother of three, who knew the struggles and pains of life. They both knew what Ana was going through, an emotional roller coaster ride of being in a non committal love, sexual relationship. They knew that Ana was chasing after a love that would never transpire. The emotional map of feelings of anger, hurt, fear, regret, love. The feelings of lustful sex, in an open door policy relationship. Ana began realizing slowly that she was losing him. He slowly began to withdraw further and further away from her. Debbie and Lucinda began encouraging her to keep a diary of what was happening in the relationship. She began writing in her journal as part of her therapy to forget him. She had come to the realization that this man was totally incapable of loving any one. He was selfish. Totally noncommittal. The signals were all there. Ana would drive her friends crazy.

Will he call me, asked Ana frantically?

Move on, they would say.

Unconditional love felt unctuous until it was lost. So many sweet-sour memories, his sexy, firm voice telling her things, seducing her.

Why did she yearn for it? The resonance of his voice and its emotional tones haunted her. Now, he's talking like that to someone else.

What did Ana want from Rick? Intimacy. Commitment. But he couldn't deliver anything but counterfeit concern.

What else? Passion. Ana still clinged to her obsession, fearing its loss. She would call her two best friends on the phone and desperately asked for advice. She was beside herself. The unknown was creeping in on her again. The feelings of uncertainty, once again.

She began listening to motivational speakers, Anthony Robbins, was one of her favorites. The encouragement and inspiration kept her going. Rick was hovering on her mind. She was still obsessed with him. She still wanted and desired him. Her mind would wander back to the times in the car that they made passionate love. The times that she would rub the strawberry cream, the sweat pouring down his face and dripping on to her firm, large breasts. Rick loved her pencil eraser shaped nipples. The thrust of his body against hers. The Roman candle dripping on his body. Ana had to stop thinking about him, it was driving her crazy.

She buried herself in her work and kids. She had to stop with the self-blame. Rick was just a selfish, immature, asshole. He needed therapy. Now she understood why his wife had left him, his inattentiveness drove her to seek comfort in the arms of another man. Ana felt that perhaps she could persuade him to forget about that dreadful night. The night that he walked in and found his wife in bed with her boyfriend Matthew.

Always shift blaming others for his under achievements. His defense was always to blame others. Never soul searching within his own flaws. His behavior was typical of a neurosis character. He was incapable of holding onto a woman. A caveman, a typical hunter. It was time Ana felt that she should confront him. Oh God, give me courage. Ana decided the time was right. He ignored her phone calls. She knew that he was being a coward. She waited for him after work. She waited until he was inside his car. She was parked alongside of him.

I need to talk to you, she said.

About what?

About my life.

Alright, said Rick.

He slowly walks to her car and sits in the passenger side and finally had the courage to confront him. Where is this relationship going? A moment's silent. His left leg began to shake, clearing his throat.

I told you a long time ago I wasn't looking for a relationship. I like to be free to roam.

What are you telling me that you want to be with other women?

No!

I've been married before.

I felt like an animal in a cage.

I've been in a relationship where I almost lived with a woman.

So, what you are saying is you're never getting married?

I didn't say never.

He Never Called Again

I'm not planning on getting married now.

I can't believe you said the M word.

Yes, I did.

I was just asking a question.

I just wanted to know where this was going, and you told me everything.

How you really feel.

You have played me like a fine guitar.

Ana's heart dropped. She wanted to be strong. Ana tried to remain composed however the tears began falling down her face. She lost it. He never loved me, she thought. Ana sucked in her breath and stared at him while her emotions ranging from shock to fury, to hurt, charged through her.

What did you say?

She couldn't believe what she was hearing. She began to cry, it was the first time he ever saw her cry.

Backing away, afraid that she was going to punch him out, she felt like slapping him, even go as far as scratching his eyes out. Her heart was pounding so hard. She paused, she tried to compose herself, and she said I'm being so emotional. Rick's eyes became narrowed, and his features took on the hardness of a perfect shaped diamond on a Mohr's scale. He had mangled her heart emotionally and mentally. He made a fool of her; he used her as a doormat. She could never forgive him. The silence built. You lied to me, you used me. You encouraged me.

I should have never spoken to you, he responded.

I should have ignored you.

She wanted revenge. The feelings of love and hate, so confused. She had above average intelligence, how she thought could she be in love with a man like him. He didn't respect her. Ana felt betrayed and used.

I am not a masochist, she thought.

The pay back is a bitch, said Ana. Deeply and profoundly saddened Ana's heart was crushed, she turned away. She jumped in her car and took off in a frenzy. She had to move on. Ana had to walk away from the relationship that was destroying her. The very next day emotional crushed she turned to Debbie for hope and words of encouragement. Ana was devastated. The hour long telephone conversation with Debbie made her realize that it was Rick's loss and he had the emotional problems. He was incapable of love. Ana was deeply attracted and vulnerable to Rick's needs. Ana's need for attachment and dependency complimented Rick's desire for detachment and autonomy. Ana perceived Rick as all giving and benevolent, and he perceived her as all taking and malevolent. It wasn't until that day that Debbie said something that made Ana snap out of it. She mentioned his way of thinking reminded her of Charles Manson. She thought he was a serial killer.

Rick is not a serial killer.

He's not capable of killing anyone.

A few weeks later Ana walked in the library, and it was at that moment of pushing the glass door into the library that she felt something strange was happening to her again. She walked through the library and remembered the explorer rolling over again. Something inside her began to change. She no longer cared if he ever called her again. She felt a transformation.

Was it a miracle? Was it something magical that she felt was transpiring in her, perhaps a spiritual awakening? Ana began on a quest, somehow when she entered the library; she felt a strong sensation, a renewed spirit coming inside of her. She felt like a heavy load was lifted from her. Was this a sign? Ana still felt love for Rick, even though her heart was broken into tiny pieces. She didn't feel she was obsessed by him, anymore.

She felt a certain special love, a love that was unexplainable. She felt a sort of rejuvenation, a recharging of her batteries. She began working on herself to become the kind of partner that she wanted in return. She began making a long list of attributes that she liked in her partners. Ana began studying the list carefully, and paring the numbers down to about twelve qualities that she felt was essential. Then she began the process of reviewing the list again to see if she had the qualities that she was seeking in someone else. Ana created an open space in her life for that special person to come in by freeing herself from the dead end relationship.

It was the following Sunday morning, that Ana walked in to St. Andrew's Church, with her eyes fixed on the images of Christ, piercing all the visions of the places that he dragged his cross, she felt a chill that was beyond words. She kneeled in the first pew, facing and staring at every detail of the Statue of Our Lady of Fatima, when she began to pray.

At last she found a place she can turn too for spiritual guidance. She felt the silence of the Church, she felt the silence of the people around her, some praying, some reading the missal book, some praying the rosary, Ana felt she found a place of peace. A place she felt strong and confident. It was sometime after the first gospel that Father Mark, gave his interpretation. Suddenly it became very clear as if it was a sign, as if he was directly speaking to her. He began saying that everyone is a pearl, the pearl of great price. What does that mean? Ana thought.

He began saying that in relationships we sometimes pray to God for the relationship to work, instead of asking for enlightenment and opening our hearts to the right person. We ask for that special person we love to marry us. A year later, because we didn't leave it to the higher power, couples find themselves in that dream that turned into a nightmare. They are miserable. Father Mark continued in his enlightening sermon. I can't believe he is saying this, Ana thought. Instead of praying for this person to marry us, ask to open up our hearts, and lead us to the right person. She could not believe what she was listening too, the meaning of the pearl of great price.

Ana had to feel gratitude to her Higher Power, she knew somehow her perfect mate was on the way. Ana's spirit was working in her life. It was an inside-out process of looking at who she was and what she wanted to do in her life. A sense of direction. She needed to be focused in knowing what she really wanted. Ana knew that in her heart, that someday he would regret everything. Perhaps someday Rick would realize that she was the best thing that ever happened in his life, but then it would be too late. Ana was hurt, emotionally destroyed. She did have hope, and faith, and was a firm believer, that you can't lose what never belonged to you.

She began to feel a sense of relief as if she was surrendering herself to a Higher Power. It felt like a mystifying, metaphoric tranquility of Zen. She felt relaxed in going through the graces of identifying and living her own values.

Lost souls. A love for mankind. She felt determined to spread love, a strong determination to go on a mission of universal love. Ana's inner beauty began to unfold. She began to interact with the world, by sharing, and doing small acts of kindness. When she gave to those outside her immediate circle, she became a richer human being. Ana became a generous and compassionate person; she didn't expect anything back from others. She realized that if she gave with no strings attached, her giving would always be rewarded. She knew that it may not be returned in the same source, or in the same way, but return it would. Her life seemed to hold a greater purpose when she helped someone else.

Ana took the time to appreciate life; she began to smile at the elderly people in her neighborhood. Driving to work, she allowed herself an extra five minutes for the commute, so she could let other drivers have the right of way on occasion. She came to the realization that by giving a few minutes of her time a day, it had a profound impact on people's lives, as well as hers. Ana began to wear a smile on her face, even though at times it still hurt inside. She knew that it had a ripple effect, for those that came in contact with her, and experienced her friendliness they felt better. And they passed it on. Sometimes she was totally astonished on how much one smile would do for the world.

She needed that spiritual inspiration, every Sunday, to keep her going for the work week. Ana felt strength when she began to reach out and help someone else.

She became active in the parent's group at her children's school. She looked out for the elderly woman who lived next door to her and offered her a ride whenever she went grocery shopping at times.

The following Monday, the sunlight streamed through the window of Ana's office warming her neck. She closed her eyes and fantasized that everything was all right, and there is always a reason for everything. Destiny. Fate. She knew deep down inside her, that this too shall pass. Whenever she began to feel sad, she would remember that nobody could make you feel inferior or depressed unless you allowed it.

Ana continued researching in the library the psycho analysis of a deranged mind. The checklist that summarizes the mind of a psychopath. The fascinating and distressing problems of the human mind. She began to research more, the books she brought home to read intrigued her. Ana began taking mental notes one in thirty men are sociopaths, an estimated 3 percent of our male population. The profile of the psychopath, superficial charm with glibness. The manipulation and conning, never recognizing the rights of others and see themselves as self serving. The lying and lack of remorse, shame or guilt. The shallow emotions, the incapacity for love. Ana couldn't believe what she was reading. The behavioral problems, the promiscuous sexual behaviors, the early behavior problems. She had become fascinated.

What causes people to be like that?

Why? Ana wondered. She researched and continued to read more; the primary reasons were believed to be neurological abnormalities in the frontal lobe of the brain. The area that dealt with self- control.

The area related to fear conditioning; the reasons being were genetic, brain disease or a head injury due to an accident, perhaps a motor cycle accident. The other theory might be the upbringing, the dysfunctional family environment, abusive parents, and poor education. The conclusion was that the type of brain, the neurons one was born with and the environment in which one was born into, creates a psychopath. Ana's eyes widen as she read through the books at the library. She was in a state of confusion and disbelief.

Oh My God!

I am in love with a psychopath. His lack of emotional attachment was part of the psychopathic personality, a frightened five year old boy trapped in a man's body. His preconventional morality, his moodiness, his predatory lifestyle, his lack of conscience. She continued to research about the psychopathic mind, and the more she read the more she was convinced that he was a psycho. His lack of bonding.

Looking back she began to wonder, she began to analyze. Why was he afraid to commit?

She continued reading in her bedroom that evening, turning the pages slowly, in total silence. She wonders. Her eyes are becoming very heavy. She closes her eyes for a few seconds. Her eyes open again. Am I dreaming? What evil lurks in a psychopathic mind? Until that evening she hadn't been able to put her finger on where she remembered that face, the face of Dr. Walt Spellman.

Oh My God! Jesus Christ, she remembered.

Her mind racing, a state of confusion, suddenly the phone rings.........

He Never Called Again

Rose F. Quintiliano

AFTERWORD

What is a surname? It is a part of someone's life forever, it represents who we are. It's our heritage, so we can pass it along to our children and grandchildren and great grandchildren. The name Quintiliano was derived from the Latin origin.

Marco Fabio Quintiliano was one of the greatest writers of the first century. He was born 37 AD in Calahorra, Spain. He studied in Rome with the orator Domitus Afer. It was at some point later that he returned to his native land of Spain. He was the first rhetorician to receive a salary from the state, known then as the fiscus. He opened his own school, where he taught for twenty years. He was made tutor to Domitian's nephews and heirs, the son's of Flavius Clemens, through whom he gained the ornamenta

He Never Called Again

consularia. It was in 88, that he retired to write his masterpiece, Institutio Oratoria. His death is unknown, but it is believed to be somewhere in the 90's.

Therefore, I am deeply indebted to so many people who have written about him.

But above all, I am indebted to the people of Calahorra, Spain, for keeping his memory alive.

Muchas Gracias,

Rose F. Quintiliano

Rose F. Quintiliano

ABOUT THE AUTHOR

Rose Quintiliano, works for a major airline and has been writing for many years. *He Never Called Again* is her first published book. Rose lives in New Jersey with her family.

Printed in the United States
15900LVS00001B/73-75